The Other Side of Yesterday

The Other Side of Yesterday

Dorothy Martin

MOODY PRESS

CHICAGO

©1978 by

THE MOODY BIBLE INSTITUTE
OF CHICAGO

ISBN: 0-8024-6095-X

Printed in the United States of America

ONE

Long after the danger and terror were over, the mournful wail of the foghorn or the sound of water lapping against rocks brought Katie memories of the net of suspicion and intrigue that had tightened around her so suddenly.

It had all started that hot day in the public library where she worked part-time to put herself through graduate school. The heat and commotion of people had battered her that day as she automatically reached for library cards, inserted date-due slips in book pockets, and tried to smile at the fretful, perspiring faces that came and went.

The old, stately library building, blackened by long years of coal smoke, was a landmark on the downtown corner, with the business section bustling around it. It was an original building that dated back to the city's early pride in its cultural heritage. Talk of tearing it down to replace it with a more modern structure never got far because of public sentiment. When the building was designed, there was no such thing as air conditioning.

5

But people became accustomed to comfort and began to complain about the stuffy building on warm summer days. Finally the city fathers had yielded and air conditioned the main reading room. Now, when it was most needed, the system had malfunctioned. All afternoon people had come to the library not for books, but hoping for a sanctuary from the unusual late-summer heat that frayed nerves and exploded tempers over trivialities.

Two groups of second-grade children swished back and forth in the early afternoon, whispering loudly. Thirty sixth-graders came just before school was out, importantly looking for material for a first research paper. They made repeated noisy trips to the drinking fountain. Later, during the afternoon story hour, a two-year-old, sent with his sister for an hour of free babysitting, cried loudly and spoiled listening for everyone.

The heat in the room boiled these ordinary annoyances into major problems.

Katie looked up at the slow-crawling hands of the big clock on the wall over the main entrance. Five minutes remained until her supper break. Even though she would have to spend most of it in the stacks taking notes for history class, it would be a welcome relief from people. This kind of day made her wonder if a master's degree was worth the struggle.

She checked out the books thrust in front of her and then slid off the high stool behind the check-out desk. She grabbed her purse and lunch sack and gave a grateful smile to the high school girl who filled

6

in over the supper hour. Threading her way between the tables to the back of the stacks, she dragged the step ladder close to the one window that would stay open without being propped up, and perched on the ladder. The forty-five minute supper break would give her just enough time to skim a mystery story and take notes on the history book on the Mexican War—one book for pleasure, one for duty.

She reached into the paper sack for the sandwich, unwrapped it, and looked at it with distaste. Usually the room was cool enough to keep the bag supper appetizing. Now she imagined she could see, under the wilted lettuce, the wiggly tails of bacteria that had feasted on the tuna filling all afternoon. She rewrapped the sandwich and wadded it back in the sack. The apple, warm instead of cold and crisp, was at least safe to eat.

Sitting with a book on her lap, her hands cupping her cheeks, she was oblivious to her surroundings as she read until a voice nearby said, "What you need is a Wednesday's child."

The voice, crisp, resonant, deep, with amusement edging it, caught Katie's attention.

She heard a muted laugh answer the words, and a soft voice asked, "*Is* there any such person left in these days of compulsive independence?"

Intrigued by the snatch of conversation from the other side of the shelves, Katie peered over the tops of the eye-level books and saw a man's broad shoulders in a plaid sport shirt. Half-standing on the ladder she caught, through the partially empty top shelf, a fleeting glimpse of a woman, her hair a silver sheen below the man's shoulder. Climbing down off the ladder, Katie stepped around the end of the row, but only a flicker of movement at the far end showed that someone had just left.

She looked at her watch then and hurriedly skimmed the last chapter of the history, making notes in her special abbreviated shorthand that would keep the main points intact until she could type the information more fully on cards.

She shoved the history book back in place and started back to work but could not resist dipping into books here and there as she passed them. She read the beginning and end of a current best seller, and grimaced at the language and descriptions. Finally she turned reluctantly toward the checkout desk and then remembered her notes. Rushing back to the history section, she pulled the book out and impatiently shook it, alert to Miss Elder, whose mind clocked minutes more accurately than a stopwatch. The papers fluttered to the floor, and as she leaned to pick them up, she bumped into an old gentleman who was sitting near her at a table. His overhanging white eyebrows bristled, and he frowned at her as he rattled his newspaper irritably.

"Sorry," she mouthed and stuffed the notes into her purse on the way back to the front desk.

Shaping her lips into a smile at Miss Elder, she slipped into her place as the room began to fill with the evening crowd. Behind the smile she nodded in answer to "Ain't it hot!" and "Did you hear this heat wave is supposed to last all week?" and "Why don't you do something about the terrible heat in here?"

8

She thinned her lips into a tight line to keep from snapping back at the last complaint from a too-fat woman in a sleeveless dress. Anyone complaining about the heat in this building should see the airless rooms at the top of Mrs. Ireland's house where she and five other girls also struggling for master's degrees stood in line for the bath.

While one part of her mind kept her hands reaching mechanically to check books in and out, another part was alert to titles she needed for information for several papers and for her thesis. It saved her time at the card catalog if she jotted down information as books were returned. This evening several of them looked promising, and she listed titles and authors and brief descriptions on cards in the little, abrupt, boxlike lines that were her shorthand symbols.

At the same time, words she had overheard teased the fringe of her memory. *Wednesday's child.* She frowned as she puzzled over them. How did that little ditty go? *Wednesday's child was—something.*

It had been one of her grandmother's sayings. The words brought a picture of herself standing on a chair by a kitchen table with one of Grandmother's over-the-head aprons wrapping her as she carefully cut out slender rings of dough.

Wednesday's child is—kind? No. Wednesday's child is—lovely? No, lov—loving and—something else. Her mind worried it, turning the words over and over. *Loving and giving.* That was it. Now that she had the momentum, perhaps she could carry it on. *Wednesday's child is loving and giving, Thursday's child is—is—works—works hard for a living.*

9

She did not realize that she had said the last words out loud triumphantly, until the man standing at the desk said a startled, "What's that?"

Katie looked up into dark blue eyes under thick, blond eyebrows that were drawn together in a straight line as he stared down at her and at the clutter on the desk.

Trapped in a moment of embarrassment, Katie floundered for an explanation, knowing that one was not necessary but giving it anyway under the compulsion of the intent look in his dark blue eyes.

"N-nothing. Just—something my grandmother used to say."

"What made you think of it now?"

Not knowing what to answer, she took the three books he handed her and checked them, purposely not looking at the name on the library card he gave her.

As she pushed the books back across the desk to him he said, "I was curious, because my grandmother used to say the same thing, and I wondered if we could be related."

Katie looked up at him. Hearing the laughter coloring his voice and seeing the smile lifting the edges of his mouth, she gave a slow smile in return. "No, but our grandmothers are probably from the same century," she answered gravely.

He laughed down at her then and stood looking at her. The expression in his eyes was warm, friendly, and admiring. Confused by his attention, she looked down at the cards with her notes and saw how silly the markings looked, as though she had been doodling. She reached self-consciously and turned the cards over. He looked at them too, smiled at her, and picked up his books. Watching him leave, she noticed the erectness of his broad shoulders in the plaid sport shirt as he pushed through the outer door. No wonder he had been startled at her words. He was the one in the stacks a couple of hours earlier who had talked about Wednesday's child. He was responsible for the trail of memory that had taken her back to the warmth of a kitchen that snowy winter day long ago when she had carefully cut out doughnut rings knowing nothing of the battle her mother was losing with cancer.

Through the rest of the busy evening, her mind worried the little refrain. There were other lines to it, something for each day of the week. She tried to remember what they were as she walked home through the closeness of the late summer evening.

It was still light enough that she felt safe on the streets, but in a few weeks it would be dark long before the library closed. She dreaded the thought of walking home alone in the deserted streets of the cold winter darkness. Even thinking about it now made her quicken her steps and hurry the last block to the walk leading up to Mrs. Ireland's worn house with its yard patched by clumps of grass. At other houses along the block people sat in their yards in friendly dismay at the heat or on front steps to catch whatever stray breeze drifted by. But Mrs. Ireland's front yard and steps were empty.

"You're paying for the privilege of room and bath, nothin' else," was her tight-lipped order. "I don't hold

11

with a lot of sittin' around, wasting time. If you've got a young man, let him come and get you and bring you back. I don't want them around in the way other times."

There was no longer a Mr. Ireland. Her roomers claimed it was because she had the same rules for him.

Katie climbed the two flights of uncarpeted stairs. She already knew how to avoid the most creaky boards. Heat hung blanketlike over the two single beds in the low-ceilinged room at the top of the house. Jane sat cross-legged on one narrow cot, doing her nails; her thin pajama top clung damply to her slender shoulders and lifted slightly when the fan on the dresser turned, whirling warm air past her.

She looked up at Katie. "This heat won't last, you know. It can't!" She lifted her arm from her bare leg and wiped its dampness with the end of the patched sheet. "It's never been so hot in September. It's against tradition. The city's reputation as a haven from the heat is at stake. That's a quote from Mark," she added unnecessarily. "He grew up in this place, you know, and says it's never been like this."

"I know. Everyone claims that." Katie rubbed the back of her neck, lifting her damp hair in a tired gesture. "Maybe the heat will break before morning. I think a storm is coming. I could hear something rumbling off in the hills as I came home."

Jane looked up at her in surprise. "How come you're so hot? Didn't you soak up some cold air in the library?"

"No, something was wrong with the air condition-

12

ing, and we all baked. Everyone snapped at everyone else. Even the little mousey man who comes in to do the floors bared his teeth at the kids. To think I used to *want* to be a librarian. That's when I thought all you did was sit and read all the books."

Katie sat down on the floor in front of the open window. The conversation with the man in the library came back to her. "I guess I'm destined forever to be a Thursday's child."

"What's that?"

" 'Thursday's child works hard for a living.' "

Jane frowned. "Why just Thursday children?"

"That's a quote. Haven't you ever heard it?"

"Uh-uh. You know math and chemistry are my corner. Mark's the one who knows things to quote. But he's never used that one. How does it go?"

Katie dug under her bed for the box of books she had to keep for use but had no room to put out on the meager two-shelf bookcase Mrs. Ireland allowed each room. She pulled out her well-thumbed Bartlett's *Familiar Quotations*, ran her finger down the index, and flipped to the page listed.

"Here it is. Listen and be literate."

> Monday's child is fair of face,
> Tuesday's child is full of grace,
> Wednesday's child is loving and giving,
> Thursday's child works hard for a living,
> Friday's child is full of woe,
> Saturday's child has far to go.
> But the child who is born on the Sabbath day
> Is brave and bonny and good and gay.

13

She closed the book and looked across at Jane who repeated, " 'The Sabbath day.' That's Sunday?"

Katie nodded.

Jane waved one hand. "Don't worry about it, then. I was born on Sunday, and I'm none of those things."

Katie smiled at the no-nonsense tone of voice she had discovered Jane always used to cover sentiment. "You're a big fake, you know. I've only roomed with you a couple of weeks, but I know you're a pushover when someone needs help. Even though it doesn't show on the surface."

"Nuts! I'm as hard as nails."

"I still remember Mark's standing behind me in line waiting to register for class. He looked over my shoulder and knew I needed a place to live because I hadn't put an address on my card. He said his girl needed a roommate, someone to look after her. When I met you I was sure I'd come to the wrong place because you were Miss Efficiency personified that day."

"I still am," Jane answered calmly.

"Sure! With bread crumbs in your pockets to feed the pigeons and money in your bag to buy milk for stray cats." Katie stopped herself from adding, *And your notebook full of papers you typed for Mark and your arms loaded with shirts you washed and ironed for him.*

"I always did like to take care of things—birds with broken wings, a dog with an injured paw, kids with skinned knees."

Katie looked at Jane as she sat absorbed in applying nail polish. Did she know what she was saying?

14

That helpless description fit Mark. Katie thought about him. He was tall and gangly. His glasses always needed to be pushed up from where they had slid down his narrow nose. A serious person, he read constantly, even while going from one class to another; some invisible antennae kept him from bumping into walls and people. He was nice, of course, but so—ineffectual. In the brief weeks Katie had known them, she had often wondered what attracted brilliant, clever Jane to Mark. Apparently it was this response to something helpless.

Katie smiled at Jane affectionately. "You're Wednesday's child." At Jane's questioning look she explained, "Loving and giving."

"No, no. I'm just being practical. If I didn't type Mark's papers and correct them, they'd be a mess. He needs looking after."

"And having his decisions made for him?"

"I don't *make* them. But we do talk things over. Mark's so impractical. He puts his nose in a book and can't see beyond it. But he's good at figuring out things. I guess because he reads so much." She looked at Katie. "You can laugh now, because you're not dating anyone. Just wait until you fall in love, and then you'll want to do things for your man too."

Katie was silent as she watched Jane move around the room laying out her clothes for the next day and stacking books and papers in a neat pile. Anyone could tell she loved Mark, but the way she showed it somehow made him seem younger than she, dependent on her.

"The man I fall in love with has to be strong

15

enough for *me* to lean on. I don't want someone I have to constantly remind to—to put on his rubbers."

She said the words impulsively, and Jane exclaimed, "Katie!" Her voice was hurt and angry. "I can't help it if I fuss over Mark. He takes cold so easily and he is so absentminded. I'm not bossing him around just because I remind him about things. That's just—well, that's just *caring* about him and showing it."

"Oh, Jane, I'm sorry. I didn't mean that personally. You're right, of course." She waved one hand in a futile gesture. "This whole business of what women should be or not be is confusing. It pulls in both directions. And both of them are right—partly at least. But women shouldn't be *more* any more than they should be *less*."

She faced Jane across the cramped room. "I shouldn't be arguing with you about this. You've found your future with Mark, and it's just what you want. But here I am stuck in this attic, a whole year away from my degree, and scratching for every penny just to survive." She added, her voice rueful, "And nobody even gives me a chance to tell him to wear his rubbers."

"Because *you* don't give anyone that chance," Jane retorted. "There are a lot of men who would date you if you looked at them for a moment. A girl like you who walks in beauty ought to have been snatched up long before you ever got to the place of working on a master's degree in history."

Katie stared at her. " 'Walks in beauty'?" she repeated. The words sounded unfamiliar coming from Jane.

"Mark again. A quote, isn't it? From a poet or someone?" She looked across at Katie speculatively. "He's right, you know. He says you have a luminous quality, whatever that means. I told him it's because you're working too hard and not getting enough to eat. That gives you this translucent look. You know—deep, wide eyes with shadows smudged under them and hollow cheeks. I should make you take vitamins. I'll give you some from that big bottle I got for Mark."

Katie, curious, asked, "You don't mind Mark's quoting poetry about some other woman?"

"Mind? No! Not about you. I can trust you. Anyway, he's always quoting poetry about something or other. Trees and rocks and stars—even the fog. Isn't there one about the fog being cat's feet? Or something like that? I don't see it myself, all that imagination. I like the two-plus-two-equals-four logic."

Katie laughed, shaking her head. "If it is true that opposites attract, you and Mark are going to have a perfect marriage."

"You should look for an opposite too," Jane retorted. "Find a man who is tall for your five feet, big for your littleness, light-hearted for your seriousness, with blue eyes and blond hair to contrast with your deep brown hair with its copper lights—"

Katie laughed again and reached to snap off the light. "OK, OK! Go ahead and arrange Mark's life if you want to, but leave mine alone."

She lay still in the heated dark. Jane's words

17

brought to mind the image of the man in the library with his tall strength, deep voice, and direct, dark blue gaze. He seemed to admire her as a person and not just someone hired to stamp cards for borrowed books. The heat made her restless. She turned, pushed back the weight of the sheet, and turned her damp pillow over. How silly to think about someone she would never see again. And someone who would never give her a second thought if they did meet again. She was acting like an adolescent with a crush on a handsome face.

Walks in beauty. She smiled over the words. At least for now she would have to settle for Mark's description, nice even though it was not true and from a man who already belonged to someone else.

TWO

The exhausting heat lasted two more days, but was made bearable for Katie because the library air conditioning system was repaired. However, the stifling atmosphere of the small room at the top of Mrs. Ireland's house drained her energy, making it hard to face the hours she needed to study when she got home from work. The wearing heat made her nerves jumpy too. Her imagination heard furtive footsteps behind her as she hurried home Friday from the library.

The thunder that had rumbled somewhere off in the hills for several days still threatened a storm. An occasional jagged streak of lightning briefly illumined the trees and bushes, making the darkness seem more intense by contrast. The distance between the library and Mrs. Ireland's house, so familiarly safe in the daytime, was spooky after dark. She had to force herself to walk calmly up the porch steps and into the narrow hall without running the last few steps.

The unreasonable panic had lifted by the time she

19

climbed the worn steps to the crowded room at the top of the house and smiled a tired greeting at Jane.

She dropped her purse and books in a heap on the cot and looked down at the week's shorthand notes that were waiting to be translated into sensible words if she could make the frayed typewriter ribbon hold out long enough.

"Jane, any chance of using your typewriter? This ribbon is practically holes."

"I'm sorry. Mark borrowed it. But he's bringing it back tomorrow."

"Good excuse not to do these notes tonight. They can wait until I buy a new ribbon tomorrow. I'll have time Sunday to type them."

It was almost noon when she awoke Sunday and saw the note Jane had left propped against the lamp.

"Gone on a picnic with Mark. Left you an orange and a doughnut and a Vitamin A."

Katie stretched her arms over her head, luxuriating in feeling rested. It was cooler now that Saturday's storm had passed through and sent slanting sheets of rain to knock leaves from trees and beat them into sodden heaps along the sidewalks.

She got up and took advantage of the empty bathroom to take a leisurely bath, using a few drops of the bath oil Mark had given Jane for a birthday present. Katie's lips quirked in a smile as she remembered Jane's analyzing the contents in the lab and telling Mark he had wasted his money because she could have concocted something just as effective a lot cheaper in the lab at school.

Later, with a cup of coffee made with water from

the hot water faucet in the bathroom, she stood by the narrow window under the sloping roof, sipping the weak, lukewarm brew. The window looked out on a narrow, dirty alley lined with garbage cans which were an open invitation to stray cats looking for dinner.

The friendly town she had come from loomed suddenly before her, and her throat tightened with longing to be back there. She saw the open space surrounding it where one could look in any direction and see the distant melting of sky into ground that gave a feeling of infinity. She felt again the protecting closeness of belonging to people who had known her parents and grandparents and who had given loving support to a widowed professor and a mother-less child. The warmth of belonging had woven a shelter of security she ached for now. Was there ever anywhere a balance between dependence and inde-pendence? If only one could move like a circle within a circle, alone and yet not alone.

She had come away from the familiar town be-cause it offered no opportunity to get the degree she needed. The university here did. Leaning against the window frame, Katie thought about the city's reputa-tion. The summer months made it a haven for hay fever sufferers and for campers who came for the beauty and solitude of the woods that lay at the edge of civilization. But winter months brought only those outsiders in whom cold and deep snows aroused a deep primeval urge to conquer wilderness.

Geography had dictated the city's development from its beginnings along the edge of the lake.

Houses and businesses stretched in a thin line along the shore for forty miles. Then the city left the lake's edge and crept up the hillsides. Its steep streets were the delight of sledding children in winter and the despair of motorists pushing hard on brakes. She was a transient in a city plastered against a hill and bordered by a lake that controlled its people's industry, weather, and temperament.

Katie turned from the window abruptly. Dwelling on another place and time and people was futile. Somehow she must get through this year's heavy load of work and study and get a degree on which to build future security.

She straightened the cardboard under the short leg of the table that served as desk, table, and ironing board, and looked at the stack of books and papers. She felt empty and alone. It would be fun to be on a picnic with someone who shared both memories and dreams. What she had told Jane was true. No one had ever dated her seriously either in high school or in college. College men had talked to her in class, come to the house to visit, taken her to school events. But none had ever seemed interested in more than a passing friendship. And she had not met anyone she liked well enough to want to know better.

Free and easy repartee had never come naturally for her as it seemed to for some girls. The ability to date casually eluded her. She always felt the involuntary stiffening of her shoulders, a pulling away from instead of melting into an embrace. It was the vivid memories of the exclusiveness of love she had seen in her parents as a small girl that made this reaction, she was sure. Love did not come from a casual shopping around. But now it would be fun to know someone special.

Her thoughts broke off as she pulled typewriter and books closer impatiently. She had to get to the least interesting but most necessary part of her study routine and transfer into sense the cryptic notes she made on her reading. She rolled in the first card to begin the uneven typing rhythm that was a drawback whenever she applied for an office job.

But almost immediately she leaned back against the chair, her fingers resting on the keys as she frowned down at the notes she had shaken from the history book. They were on the same kind of plain, lined notebook paper she always used, but the notes were not hers. She got up and carried them to the window to see them better. They were not her odd symbols, but neither were they the swoops and curves of conventional shorthand. The few words interlacing the symbols didn't make sense even though they looked like a kind of scrambled English.

She studied the pages, wondering where they had come from. How had they got into her purse? She thought back to that stifling Wednesday evening when she had made the notes. They were supposedly those on the last two chapters of the British historian's assessment of the Mexican War. Then what had happened? She had heard the snatch of words about Wednesday's child—

"No, that came first, while I was reading." She said the words out loud as she tried to reconstruct the scene.

She had heard the voices and tried to see who was talking. Then she had found that her supper break was almost over. She had started back to the desk where Miss Elder sat looking over the tops of her glasses and clocking Katie's tardy return to work. Discovering she did not have her notes, she had gone back and pulled the book out quickly and shaken it; her notes had fallen to the floor. Only they were not hers. She had grabbed up the papers and accidentally knocked against the little old man who in turn had glared at her. She had stuffed the pages in her shoulder bag and had not looked at them until now.

She walked back and tossed the sheets on the table. She put her hands on her hips, and her eyebrows came together in a disgusted frown. She could only hope her notes were still in the book. If not, she would have to reread the chapters. The material would certainly be a part of the exam, and that class was too important to risk getting a low grade.

But that would mean several hours of time she did not have. If she could just do a little studying during work when Miss Elder was away, she would have the needed time. But she had heard her dad's old-fashioned axiom, "Do an honest day's work for an honest day's wage," too often to ignore it. Well, if she got to the library early tomorrow—skip lunch maybe, and eat an extra sandwich for supper—there would be time to redo the notes.

She dropped the gibberish into the wastebasket and then, on impulse, reached down and pulled the papers out. Jane was a puzzle fanatic. Maybe she would be able to figure out if this was childish practicing of the alphabet with the letters all strung together repeatedly or a private love note someone had put in the book on a prearranged plan. If so, she had better put it back whether she found her notes or not.

Monday's bright, cool sunshine helped get the week started. Every nice day was a bonus because she could walk the two miles from campus to the library and save bus fare for the city's winter days of deep snow and bitter cold. All too soon the city's winter gloom would burden them.

Today she walked quickly, enjoying the red and gold leaves clinging stubbornly to tree branches. But when she reached the big, blackened building, her feet moved slowly up the wide front steps and stopped outside the door. She was reluctant to leave the crisp air and bright sun for the dark mustiness of the old building. What if she were to march in and say, "Let's put a table outside and check out books there. It would bring us a rush of business."

Miss Elder would raise her eyebrows indignantly as she looked over the tops of her glasses and snapped her lips in a thin line. "*Miss* Cameron, what an *impossible* idea. Why, those tables are too *heavy* to move. And how *could* we carry all the books out?"

When I'm old, I'm going to think young! Indignant at the imaginary conversation, Katie pulled open the door, marched in without a glance at Miss Elder, and went back to the stacks.

She reached confidently for the book. It was not there. She hunted along the shelf, thinking it must

25

have been used and not put back in the right place. Not finding it, she went to the check-out desk and riffled through the cards. No one had taken it out either.

She walked back and searched the shelves again, by now annoyed and determined to find the book, if not the notes. The trouble with people was that they were so careless, putting books back on the shelves anywhere, not caring if it was the correct place. She felt silly pulling one book after another off the shelf and peering behind each, and she looked around self-consciously. The few people at nearby tables were busy with their own affairs, not watching her.

She found the book on a shelf below where it should have been, hidden behind two others. She pulled the book down and thumbed the pages until she found her notes. She slipped them deep into her shoulder bag with a sigh of relief that she would not have to reread the book's detailed analysis and many fine-print footnotes. Book titles caught her attention as she browsed along the shelves on her way back to the front desk. Finally at three o'clock she slipped reluctantly into her place on the high stool and braced herself for the after-school rush.

She reached automatically for the six paperbacks and library card someone laid in front of her. When she saw the book titles, she smiled up at the young man.

"Apparently you are a science-fiction fan."

He grinned back at her. "I eat 'em up."

"Too much at once could give you indigestion," she retorted.

He laughed, frankly appraising her with his light blue eyes. "You aren't the image of the stern, forbidding, old-maid librarian I remember from my childhood." He shot a mischievous, meaningful look at Miss Elder sitting in the glassed-in office with her back to them.

"*Old-maid* is a no-no word," Katie said with mock seriousness. "Would *you* want to be called a leftover just because no one was perceptive enough to see your value?"

He held up a hand in appeal. "My apologies!" He looked again at Miss Elder, her thin shoulders stiffly erect over her work, and then leaned his elbows on the desk, studying Katie's face. "Seriously, I haven't seen you around here before."

"And I haven't seen you getting books before either, so we're even."

"Yes, but you see, there's no reason for you to remember me, while I couldn't forget you after seeing you once. You haven't worked here very long, have you?"

"Only a few weeks," she answered and looked up at him. The laughter in his eyes and the crooked grin on his lips lighted his face with a friendly expression. His thick, very blond hair worn low on his forehead curled up slightly at the collar of his open-neck shirt. She slipped the card into the pocket of the top book, and gave a quick glance at his name. "Barry" was all she had time to read without giving away what she was doing.

As she shoved the books toward him, she said,

27

"Obviously you've also been reading how-to books on Irish blarney."

"No, no!" he protested. "Blarney implies something false. I'm talking from the Scandinavian honesty that I inherited. I meant what I said. Who could forget your pretty face at the desk after—" He stopped and then, the sparkle in his eyes belieing the words, he finished, "After being used to a more mature face," and looked again in Miss Elder's direction.

Katie expected any minute to hear the raspy clearing of her throat that Miss Elder thought was a tactful signal that Katie was talking too long to a customer. This time she did not even look around.

Katie listened as Barry's light, amused voice went on. "I've got another gift. I can tell what a person is like by what he carries in his pockets."

"You're safe this time. I don't have any pockets."

"Well, purses or whatever you women call them, of course. Look at me." He pulled out a pen, a comb, a handful of change, a key ring, a wallet, a couple of shells. He looked at her. "See? No cigarettes. No pills. What does that tell you about me?"

"That you won't die of lung cancer."

"Come on! It should tell you that I'm a clean, trustworthy, upstanding young man."

He waited while she checked out books for several others and then leaned on his elbows again and smiled down at her, his blue eyes coaxing. "It's your turn now. Show me what's in your purse and I'll tell you what you are like."

"If you think you can find out that easily where I live

28

and who I am, you've been too long in a fantasy world," she said, tapping his books. "And I am supposed to be working right now."

He shook his head in mock disgust. "I'm slipping. That gimmick has always worked before." He straightened and smiled down at her. "I'll be back. I'm a fast reader." He picked up his books, strode to the door, and turned to wave at her over his shoulder as he went out.

As books were shoved back and forth across the desk, Katie went over the ridiculous conversation in her mind, laughing in spite of herself. The image of his contagious smile and the laughing light in his vivid blue eyes came back repeatedly.

She had just returned from her supper break spent in the stacks with an open book on her lap, when she heard a soft voice.

"Here's Wednesday's child."

Katie turned from going over the list of overdue books and stared at the couple standing at the desk. A slender, silver-haired woman was smiling at her. Beside her stood the man in the plaid sport shirt, this time wearing a gray business suit and tie. It somehow changed his appearance from a relaxed, casual person who might be a friend to a remote businessman.

"I told my aunt about our conversation the other evening and she wanted to meet you."

Katie stared up at him. It was not just his appearance that was different; it was his attitude as well. The warmth he had shown the other time was gone. Instead his intensely blue eyes were distant, his voice aloof as he spoke quickly with no friendliness evident. His words came with clipped abruptness.

"This is my aunt, Mrs. Arne Sieverson, and I am Andrew Sieverson. We have asked questions about you and have found that you are Katherine Cameron, known as Katie. You are in the master's program at the university, majoring in history. You are hoping to teach eventually."

His aunt broke in with a quick, bright smile, her voice light. "Like all Thursday's children, you are working hard for a living."

Katie stared from one to the other, feeling a rush of uneasiness. "How did you— Who told you—" She took several steps backward, away from them.

She watched Mrs. Sieverson put a protesting hand on her nephew's arm as he started to answer, and listened as she said contritely, "I'm sorry, my dear! That was not the right way to begin. The problem is that we really did not know how to go about this. You see, we are offering you a job."

"I-already have one."

Katie's tone, flat, disinterested, closed them off as she looked around for Miss Elder. Any other time she would be right there sending too talkative people on their way. But this time Miss Elder, hurrying from the upper level, was effusive in her greeting.

"Mrs. Sieverson! Mr. Sieverson! I did not have opportunity to *tell* you the other day when we talked briefly how *nice* it is to have you back in the city. I hope you *enjoyed* your summer. Is there *anything* I can do for you?" Her teeth clicked and flashed in a

30

smile as she hovered eagerly, her eyes darting from one to the other as she looked over the top of her glasses.

"Thank you, Miss Elder. May we borrow Miss Cameron for a moment?"

"*Certainly.* Take as *much* time as you need. I will be *glad* to take her place to help *you*."

Katie, dazed by the silkiness of Miss Elder's voice, followed the Sieversons to a corner table. She listened as Mrs. Sieverson said, "Andrew, let me explain our offer in more detail."

She turned to Katie. "Miss Cameron, we live in rather a big old house at the edge of the city. I feel lonesome in it, especially when my nephew is away on business. I've decided I would like someone to live with us and help with my correspondence in exchange for room and board. We thought it would be nice to offer the position to a student. That is why we are coming to you."

She hesitated, glanced at her nephew briefly, and then back to Katie. "Of course you would be free to come and go as you wish for school or personal activities."

"But my library job—I have an obligation here—"

"We have already asked Miss Elder if she could release you if you were willing to come with us. She was very gracious and said she was sure the university would find her someone to take your place."

Katie looked at her with new respect. Who were these people who could make Miss Elder be gracious over a disruption of her sacred schedule?

She listened as Mrs. Sieverson leaned forward

31

earnestly in apology.

"Please forgive our investigation of you. We felt we needed to inquire and know something about you before offering you the job. I'm sure you understand. Naturally you'll want to do the same for us. I can tell you that we are an old established family in the city, and almost anyone can give you a reference. Miss Elder knows us, as you saw. We have credit and charge cards that will show that we pay our bills at the stores. We are members of a church. My nephew works in a bank."

She stopped and gestured with small, capable-looking hands that wore only a simple gold wedding band. "Would you consider accepting this offer?"

"I don't know—" Katie hesitated. The idea of free room and board was tempting. But there was Jane to consider.

"I don't like to leave my roommate. We share the rent, and she might not be able to find anyone to take my place."

She looked across the table at them in time to catch the quick glance they exchanged that sent some secret message between them. That decided her, and she stood, her chin up. "I appreciate your offer, but I can't accept."

They rose too, and Mrs. Sieverson put one hand out in appeal. "Please! Don't make a hasty decision. Why not think about it a day or two and talk it over with your roommate? Or at least ask Miss Elder about us before you refuse. Come out and see the house if you like."

Though done with a light touch, her persistence

came through clearly enough to keep Katie uneasy about the offer, tempting as it seemed on the surface. She looked at them as they stood watching her. They looked respectable, but newspapers constantly carried stories of crimes done by little old ladies who seemed harmless. How could she know what really lurked behind Mrs. Sieverson's—she hunted for the right word—radiance. Especially when her apparent sweetness was in such contrast to the stern expression on her nephew's face. She thought absently that his tanned skin against his blond hair showed his vigorous good health.

They were waiting for her answer. She lifted her chin again and looked back at them.

"I'm sure the university could suggest someone to you, someone who needs financial help."

"They did. You," Mrs. Sieverson answered, her face breaking into a smile. "We inquired there about you. After my nephew had seen you here," she added hastily.

Again there was that quick exchange of glances that made Katie want to turn and run.

Mr. Sieverson took his aunt's arm in an affectionate gesture and gave a brief smile. "We don't want to pressure you, of course. I'll leave you my business card. Think the offer over a day or two."

"Well, I can do that at least." She took the business card he held out to her, said a dazed goodbye, and watched them leave. Mrs. Sieverson stopped to speak to Miss Elder. Katie looked at the address on the card. "Hillcrest, Lake Shore Avenue." It sounded impressive.

33

She stared down at the card. Free room and board—no more library hassle. Excitement beat inside her as she thought, *What unbelievable good luck!*

Then she frowned, caution overcoming the excitement. It sounded too easy. There had to be a catch in it somewhere. She would have to go slow and find out if the Sieversons really were all they claimed to be.

THREE

Katie's doubts and suspicions began to dissolve when she returned to the desk and saw Miss Elder's smile, a genuine smile overlaid with respect.

"I didn't know *you* were acquainted with the *Sieversons*!"

"I'm not. Who are they?"

"My *dear*! They are one of the *oldest* families in the city. Why, *they* were here almost before there *was* a town. Their family helped *make* it. *Wonderful* people. And they simply *pour* their lives into their church."

Katie looked at the address again. "They're rich?"

"Rich in *history* as well as *money*," Miss Elder answered. Reverence colored her voice. "And to *think* they have offered *you* a chance to *live* with them in that *magnificent* old house."

Katie did not dare ask, "They really are reputable? They don't have some hidden motive for this offer that I should know about?" The awe for the Sieverson family was too clear in Miss Elder's voice, too genuine to be doubted.

This was the reaction of everyone of whom she

35

made discreet inquiries. Even Mrs. Ireland's envious sniff and, "Them who has everything gets more," gave grudging respect.

On impulse, Katie checked the card catalog for books on the history of the area and found Sieversons listed in various ways—as important early settlers, members of the city council, and leaders of various charitable organizations. Several had held the office of Mayor. One had founded a mission for derelicts still in existence. She made a wry face at that. Philanthropy seemed to be their big thing. If there was some underlying motive for their apparent generosity, it was well hidden.

Jane insisted she would be foolish to pass up the opportunity. "Don't turn it down on my account, Katie. Sure I'll miss you. But I can think of six girls who'll jump at the chance to move in with me because of being so close to campus. And I could stand any of them even though they don't have your personality. Like Mark says, things that have a common quality seek their own kind. He means we hit it off well together."

When Katie still looked dubious, Jane added, "I'll tell you what. This is the first week in October. That leaves about two and a half months in the semester. I'll get someone to move in here to finish out the semester. You try out that place, and if you don't like it you can give notice and move back here after Christmas break. Nothing much could go wrong there in just a couple of months. It will save you a lot of money. And even if they stick you in some attic room, at *that* address an attic room is sure to be better than this." She gave a sweeping gesture around the dark room with its faded, stained wallpaper.

"You sound as though you're trying to get rid of me," Katie teased.

"Only because you're willing to pass up the chance to make it through the year financially because you think you're running out on me. What's that thing Mark says? Don't look a—"

"—gift horse in the mouth," Katie chimed in, and agreed, "Well, maybe I am being too suspicious."

Still unsure as she came home Thursday in the early fall darkness, Katie sensed stealthy movements behind her. She stopped, looking back over her shoulder. No one was there, no one she could see. In spite of the comfortable family sounds she could hear coming from houses all along the familiar street, unreasoning panic started a pulse pounding in her throat and made her mouth dry. She hurried and reached the safety of Mrs. Ireland's paint-bare front door.

I'm going to take the Sieverson offer. The decision was quick, definite. No matter what catch there might be to it, nothing could be worse than having to go home in the dark night after night with fear stepping in her footsteps.

Katie called Mrs. Sieverson and made arrangements to move Saturday afternoon.

"I *am* glad, my dear. My nephew will come by for you whenever it is convenient for you."

Though assured of a replacement for the rent, Mrs. Ireland took her loss sourly. "You'll get a taste of fancy living, and it'll spoil you when you have to get out on your own. Not that them Sieversons is so all-fired great," she said with satisfaction evident in her voice. "Oh, sure, they're rich and all that. And they do things for people. Leastwise, you see their name in the papers on big committees, always for helpin' people—they say. Naturally they get a lot of glory out of it. Nobody ever asks how much real good comes from all they *say* they do."

She stopped and frowned at Katie. "I never seen you goin' to church the weeks you been here. Them Sieversons is awful religious. She tell you that? No? Always have been. Not that that's kept 'em *all* perfect," she said, her voice still smug. "They've had their black sheep more'n some of the rest of us who ain't so rich and high-toned and church-goin'."

Katie couldn't keep the stiffness from her voice as she said, "Mrs. Ireland, unless you know something definite, it's not a good idea to hint things and attack someone's reputation by innuendo."

"Don't give me none of that educated talk, young lady. What I'm sayin' is if you've got money enough people think you're better than you are. Money talks you know. Some of us honest, hard-workin' people who ain't got it, don't get the respect we should have by rights."

She stopped. Her thin face was indignant behind her thick glasses. "Someone got the idea people like the Sieversons was great, and the idea just stuck. Once an idea gets started, it sticks even if it ain't true. Just like some jerk who tried to deadbeat his way out of payin' his bill here. Said it was a two-bit place, and he went around spreadin' a story that I didn't run a clean place. Trouble was, he'd never lived in a good rooming house."

"I'm sure he hadn't," Katie replied gravely, knowing that Mrs. Ireland would not catch the sarcasm. This jealous antagonism toward the Sieverson family made Katie perversely sure she was right to accept their offer.

She was ready with her two suitcases at the foot of the staircase in the narrow front hall when Mr. Sieverson knocked on the front door. She followed him out to the car and got in while he put the suitcases in the car trunk.

They circled past the university campus and drove along a lake road that wound in a gradual curve around an extensive wooded area. The lawns became more spacious; trees and shrubbery isolated the houses from the street and from other houses. It was a part of the city Katie had not seen in the month since coming to the university. They drove in silence until Mr. Sieverson slowed the car and turned into a wide driveway whose entrance was marked by two immense stone pillars. Katie bent to see better. She caught her breath in an exclamation of delight as she saw the stone carving on top of each pillar. The carvings were ships leaning into the wind.

"My great-grandfather's idea," he answered her exclamation. "You like ships?"

"Yes. But I've not been on them much. My father read me sea stories constantly when I was a child. His people were in the fishing business several generations back."

39

"Where?"

"Scotland. Though Dad was born in this country, he had a Scot's love—passion really—for the country of his ancestors. He knew his tartan, of course, and even had a kilt that he wore occasionally."

She could hear her nervousness reflected in the thin, high tones of her voice, and she tried to relax. "And he did love the water. That's why the ships caught my eye."

"You'll feel at home here if you inherited that liking. The lake pretty much dominates the whole area, as you will see from inside."

He pulled to a stop in front of the house and got out to come around and open the car door.

He may not like me, but he is determined to be a gentleman, Katie thought with amusement as she got out and said a dignified, "Thank you."

He unlocked the car trunk to get the suitcases while she waited, looking up at the massive house. A pulse of excitement beat in her throat. This could be either an adventure or a disaster, and she found herself hoping it would be an adventure of friendship. She walked beside him up the wide, shallow steps to the double front doors.

"Oh!" The exclamation again was involuntary as she looked at the doors. The handle of each was a replica of a small, sturdy tugboat.

"Again my great-grandfather," he explained with chill reserve still evident in his voice.

Chimes echoed from inside the house as he rang the doorbell, pulled on one of the tugboats, and motioned her inside.

40

She stepped in and knew at once what Miss Elder and Mrs. Ireland had meant when they talked, each in her own way, about the Sieversons. The wide, cool hall, the beautiful staircase rising in a graceful curve to the floors above, the polished floor, the elegant grandfather clock, and the wide hall mirror with its intricately carved border reflected the graciousness of a house on which both money and love had been lavished for generations.

Mr. Sieverson put Katie's suitcases on the stairway landing, and she was suddenly aware of their shabbiness. His voice was cool but courteous as he said, "My aunt will be here in a moment. Come into the living room."

Katie followed him across the wide hall, but stopped in the doorway, not seeing the elegance and beauty of the room but only the view. The far end of the room facing her seemed to be nothing but windows stretching from ceiling to floor and from wall to wall, windows so clear they seemed to open the room to the sky. She felt thick carpet under her feet as she walked across it, drawn to what she could see lay beyond the windows.

It was the lake—a wide, shifting expanse of blue that stretched out and out and out until it lifted to meet the lighter blue of the sky. The shining water reflected the sun like a polished mirror, shimmering lightly in spots, sinking deep in others. It was dazzling, and Katie stood still, caught in its splendor.

Transfixed by the beauty of the scene, she moved closer to the window glass. But as she looked from the shining wonder of the lake to what lay just below

41

the window, she took a quick step back into the safety of the room.

"Quite a contrast, isn't it?"

Katie swallowed and half-turned and nodded as Mr. Sieverson spoke from across the room, his eyes watchful. She looked out the window again, down from its height to the jungle of weeds and brush at the bottom of the sheer cliff along which the shore stretched. The shore was lined with jagged rocks thrusting up toward the house. Perhaps seen alone it would have been a harmless picture, though not a pretty one. But the contrast with the beauty of the sparkling water chilled Katie. Both the wonder and the terror of nature were blended in one scene.

Then Mrs. Sieverson brought the safety of the room into focus again as she came in. Her hands reached toward Katie in greeting.

"My dear, welcome. We are so glad you have decided to live with us."

Katie smiled shyly back at the warm voice, reassured by the openness of Mrs. Sieverson's face and her clear blue eyes that reflected the smile on her lips.

But she really is speaking for herself. It's obvious he isn't glad at all. The thought was certain as Katie's quick glance was met and held by his cold stare.

"Let me show you your room first of all. Andrew, bring the suitcases, will you please?"

Katie followed Mrs. Sieverson's straight, slender back up the first flight of stairs and then up still another flight. She tried to take in all she could see and feel of the deeply carpeted stairs, the mirrored walls at each landing, the grandfather clock in the downstairs hall that resounded the hour while a cuckoo clock chirped an echo from some room behind them on the second floor.

Mrs. Sieverson stopped outside a white enameled door with her hand on the blue-flowered china knob. She looked over her shoulder at Katie, the expression in her eyes slightly troubled.

"I hope you won't mind being at the top of the house."

Mrs. Sieverson stopped, and in the moment of hesitation, Katie smiled to herself. *I'll have to tell Jane I am in an attic room after all.*

She listened as Mrs. Sieverson went on, "If you don't like it, you may have a room on the second floor. But to me this one is—"

She broke off again, and then with a quick laugh, she finished, "Well, I will let you decide for yourself."

She pushed the door open and stepped aside for Katie to enter. *No attic room this.* The room was small, but it seemed all air and space and light. The wall of windows across from the door was bracketed by white louvered shutters thrown back so that the tops of the trees showed. Their leaves were scarlet with a bit of green remaining. The wind made a soft sighing sound around the eaves. A pale yellow design etched every piece of the blue enameled furniture. A low, padded-blue slipper chair rocked next to a bookcase filled with books that brought childhood memories to Katie.

She turned, her face glowing. "This is beautiful!"

She caught then that quick exchange of glances.

Mrs. Sieverson's said a triumphant, *You see? I was right,* while his, with a slight warning shake of his head said just as plainly, *Go slow. Don't believe everything you see and hear.*

The silent conversation was like a dash of cold water and angered her. She had not asked to come. They had initiated the whole idea—and had been persistent—so there was no reason for her to be on trial.

I'm going to ask flat out why they chose me.

But before she could speak, Mrs. Sieverson answered her exclamation about the room. "I am glad you like it. This room has always been my favorite. In fact, I always slept in it when I visited here as a child."

She looked around, her glance resting lovingly on each piece of furniture. Then she turned to Katie. "We will leave you so you can settle in. Dinner is at 6:30."

"But—you still haven't told me what I'm to do, what my job is."

"We will talk that over later. On Monday perhaps. Let's just spend a few days getting acquainted. When we know one another a bit, we will be able to work together better."

"That's the problem. I'm afraid you'll find I won't meet your expectations. I'm not a good typist. I should have told you that right away. And I don't take conventional shorthand."

"Well, I don't speak it either," Mrs. Sieverson answered. Laughter crinkled the edges of her eyes. "Don't worry, Katie. I am sure we will be able to work together satisfactorily."

44

"You will undoubtedly discover a great deal about each other." Andrew's expression was bland and the words harmless, but Katie was sure there was a double meaning behind them. He obviously did not trust her, did not really want her to be here. But he had agreed with the hiring arrangements from the start. Why?

She stood frowning at the door after they left, wondering if perhaps after all she should pick up her suitcases, march down the stairs after them, and tell them she had changed her mind.

Finally she shrugged off the impulse and hung her clothes quickly. She found countless narrow drawers built into one wall of the closet. She puzzled over the thought that she had seen a similar closet somewhere before, and then she remembered. This was like a ship's cabin with all the furniture built securely to withstand gale winds that might dislodge whatever was not firmly anchored and send it crashing across the room. She had noticed this feature the one time she had gone to the east coast with her father and they had toured every boat they could find. It was the summer she was twelve and she had read every sea story in the library.

Drawn tight by the knot of loneliness that could still choke her with grief, she walked over to look out the windows. If she had grown up scorning her parents as so many of her contemporaries had, she might have stood her father's sudden loss better. But they had depended on one another those years after her mother's death. Grandparents had helped at first until she was old enough to manage meals and the

45

other housework sufficient for the two of them. He had given her love but left very little money, for a professor of history in a small-town college had no chance to build much of a bank account. The driver of the car, a young college kid, had had no insurance—though no amount of money could replace what a speeding car had snatched away when a corner had been turned too quickly and someone had chanced to be in the way.

Her decision to go on for a graduate degree fulfilled a dream long held by herself and her father. But it was proving to be a hard dream to reach until this miracle offer of free board and room had come.

She drummed on the white painted windowsill as she stared out at the trees. She really had no reason, no tangible reason, for this uneasy sense that something was not quite right. One should not be suspicious of kindness, even from strangers. Her parents would have offered just such help to someone needing it.

But that thought brought a frown of doubt. It was not the kindness of the act that bothered her, but the fact that there seemed to be some hidden reason for it. She sensed it in Andrew's cold, speculative look at her. Her parents' generosity would have been completely guileless. This was not. She was sure of it. And yet, thinking back over every scrap of conversation with the Sieversons, she could not really pin down anything definite on which to base her suspicions. It was the quick exchange of looks between them and Andrew's attitude of cold suspicion of her. She would

46

simply have to keep alert and move out quickly if necessary.

She turned from the window and went in search of the bathroom. She found it charming in its shades of blue and yellow. A quick look around showed her that it would be a private bath, for hers was the only occupied bedroom on that floor. Across from her, a partly open door revealed a small sewing room with everything neatly in place.

A gong rang somewhere below. Katie took a deep breath and went down the stairs, running her hand lightly along the gleaming stair rail. The sound of voices took her to the dining room and to a new face.

She stepped hesitantly into the room, and Mrs. Sieverson turned with her warm, inclusive, welcoming smile. "Katie, this is Laila. Laila Heikkinen—Katie Cameron." She looked from one to the other. "Not only your appearance, but even your names show your distinct, different nationalities."

Katie looked at Laila's slim litheness, the flat planes of her face, her smooth, white skin, and the pale, arched eyebrows over ice-green eyes that measured her in return.

Laila gave a slow, cool smile that showed white, even teeth and said, "My name is definitely Finnish, and yours says Scotch."

Somehow the word came out sounding derogatory, and Katie stiffened, lifting her chin and trying not to show anger. "Not Scotch—Scot."

"Is there a difference?" Laila's voice was amused.

"Very definitely. A person is not a Scotchman, but a Scotsman."

Mrs. Sieverson's quick laugh interrupted. "With three nationalities here we could have some interesting discussions." She turned to Katie and explained, "Laila lives here too. We have known her family for many years."

Katie saw her smile across at Laila, and then watched, curious, as color flushed Laila's face with an angry surge of red which faded, leaving a closed-in, sullen look. She turned abruptly and went through the swinging doors into the kitchen, giving the impression that she had slammed the doors behind her.

Here's another mysterious element about this situation, Katie thought and watched Laila return pushing a tea cart with warmed plates and serving dishes.

"Katie, sit there please across from Laila."

Remembering Mrs. Ireland's contemptuous, "Them Sieversons is awful religious," Katie instinctively waited, sure someone would ask a blessing for the food. Her father on occasion had asked a blessing before meals as a man of culture who acknowledged the possibility of a supreme Being. It was Andrew who prayed before the meal now.

She felt ill at ease, not sure of her status in the house. But gradually her tension lifted and she relaxed against the high back of the chair, savoring the beauty and richness of the room. The soft lights of the glittering chandelier reflected on the fragile, stemmed glassware and highlighted the warm sheen of the polished wood between the delicate, crocheted place mats.

Mrs. Sieverson and Andrew kept a conversation

48

going over a wide range of subjects in which Laila occasionally joined. But Katie only listened, making polite responses when Mrs. Sieverson turned to include her. She needed this time to observe these people with whom she would be living, people whose lifestyle and outlook were so different from her own.

Laila was arresting only in her appearance. She was clearly out of her depth when the conversation touched on politics or current events, and she made no pretense of interest. Mrs. Sieverson made a spirited defense of her views regarding low income housing in the city, and Katie saw Andrew listening respectfully, asking questions, and making notes in quick, bold strokes.

Watching him, Katie realized he was taller than she had at first thought. He was well built; his broad shoulders and confident strength gave him a self-assured look.

He doesn't waste time wondering who he is, Katie thought, remembering the discussion in yesterday's psychology class. But then, why would he need to, a handsome man who had grown up accustomed to wealth and to the adulation of poor people like Miss Elder?

She studied Mrs. Sieverson, who sat regally at the table, her slender back not touching the chair, her manners impeccable, her youthful face framed by softly waved silver hair. Even though she had been born to wealth, she had not let it affect her concern for those without it. Katie felt herself drawn into the charm of Mrs. Sieverson's personality.

But she made herself resist. *Go slow,* her common

sense warned. *The charm and concern could be a sham. You still don't know what lies behind this seemingly gracious offer.*

One thing she was sure of. The affection between aunt and nephew was genuine. She wondered about the rest of the family, where Andrew's parents were, and whether Mrs. Sieverson's husband was dead and her children, if any, were married.

When it was time for dessert, Katie helped clear the dinner plates. Laila excused herself with a quick, "I have a date, Mrs. Sieverson. If you want to take your time, perhaps she could clear the dessert dishes." Her green eyes flicked toward Katie with a hint of malice in their depths.

"Of course, Laila. Run along. We'll see to things." Then to Andrew, "Will you join us for coffee?"

He stretched and stood up. "No. I have a lesson to study for my class tomorrow. I'll take my coffee upstairs." He put his arm affectionately around his aunt, and his smile at her was loving. Then he sobered as he looked across at Katie, his voice grave. "I hope you will believe that we really want to help you."

She stared up at him. Help her? With what? Again she had that feeling of a hidden meaning in the words in which doubt and mistrust were so clear.

Holding her coffee cup, Mrs. Sieverson stood up. "Katie, bring your coffee and come into the living room. I'm sorry we are too late this evening to see the sun setting over the lake. Do you know what a spectacular sight that is?"

"Yes. My roommate and I have been down to the lake a few times. Our room at Mrs. Ireland's is at the back of the house overlooking the alley, so we couldn't see the lake from it. The sunset is never the same, is it? It is always breathtaking, though. Jane—that's my roommate—has seen it often, because she did her undergraduate work at this university. She even quotes poetry when she sees it, usually from things Mark, her fiancé, says. Poetry is out of character for Jane."

She stopped abruptly, knowing Jane would find her chattering like this out of character for her.

Mrs. Sieverson nodded agreement. "Sometimes it is difficult to find words to describe God's work in nature. But sit here, Katie, and let's have a little chat. Tell me about yourself. Where are you from?"

Katie answered, telling about her parents, of being the long-hoped-for child, of her mother's early death, of her father's teaching at the college and his sudden death, and of the gentleness and love in her home.

Mrs. Sieverson listened, her expressive face reflecting her interest and sympathy. Katie stopped and reached to put down the coffee cup. There were things she had to know about her place in this house before she could sleep easily. She leaned forward with her hands clasped tightly in her lap.

"Mrs. Sieverson. I do appreciate your offer for me to live here, because it will save me a great deal of money. But I don't want to be under any obligation. I was not raised to take something for nothing."

She stopped and moved her hands in a helpless gesture. "I ought to have come out and looked at the situation before agreeing to move in. I can see you

51

don't really need me here." She added mentally, *And that's why I'm so suspicious of your kindness.*

"Won't you let me be the judge of that?" Mrs. Sieverson answered gently. "I do want someone to help with my correspondence. And I want more than just a secretary, a—a machine to whom I can dictate. I want someone who will be a companion, a friend, a helper."

"But you already have Laila—"

Mrs. Sieverson shook her head, and her voice was decisive. "No, not Laila. She has a full time job. Anyway, she doesn't fit the picture of an old lady's companion—sensible shoes, tailored clothes, hair drawn back in a severe bun." She laughed at Katie over the rim of her coffee cup and added hastily, "Of course I do not mean to imply that you do. Except that—" She stopped and considered Katie, her head cocked and her lips pursed. Then she finished slowly and very seriously, "No matter what, I believe you *are* a loving and giving person."

"That's just it," Katie insisted stubbornly, hearing the words. "It is simply too much of a coincidence that I overheard what your nephew said in the—"

"Do call him Andrew, Katie. That is simpler and so much more friendly."

"What he said in the library that time about your needing a Wednesday's child—"

"You did? I didn't know anyone else was back in those stuffy rows that hot day. But Andrew did say *he* overheard *you* say part of the same little verse while he was standing at the desk, and you intrigued me. Literary references are not usually picked up by the

52

young these days—Forgive me, my dear. That is one of those sweeping generalities the old make about the young. Perhaps I am thinking of Laila. She is a dear girl, but she has not had intellectual advantages."

"But it's too much of a coincidence," Katie insisted still stubborn. "I overheard what you said, and then all of a sudden you invite me to live here practically free."

"And you think life should not be so easy?" Mrs. Sieverson's voice was amused as she asked the question. Then she sobered. "We are always like that, my dear. We are so suspicious when good things happen to us. We seem so afraid of what God will do to us. John Newton wrote, "Thou art coming to a King, large petitions with thee bring; for His grace and power are such, none can ever ask too much."

Her eyes were bright as she looked across at Katie. "Are you familiar with those words?"

Katie shook her head. Her voice was still obstinately stubborn as she insisted, "I have to know that I am earning my own way."

"Is there any reason you cannot enjoy life too?" Mrs. Sieverson retorted. "I am a firm believer in the 'He who does not work should not eat' principle. But if we can work and still enjoy life, isn't that all right? Katie, have you ever thought about the fact that when God created man, His original purpose was to put the highest of His creation in a very pleasant place. It was disobedience to God that brought the thorns and thistles. They were not a part of God's plan."

She stood up and crossed to put her hands lightly

on Katie's shoulders. "Don't worry about all this, my dear. I will find enough for you to do so that you will keep your self-respect intact. But I do want you to enjoy living with us." After a moment she added, "And don't let Andrew's attitude—" Once again she stopped herself abruptly and then said quickly, "Perhaps you are not aware that he is a bank examiner."

Katie had stood also, her face on a level with Mrs. Sieverson's. She thought there was a waiting look in Mrs. Sieverson's eyes as though she expected a reaction to her words. Then after a moment Mrs. Sieverson turned away and stooped to pick up her coffee cup.

"Let me show you where things are in the kitchen in case you come down for breakfast and find no one here. We always attend church. Andrew goes in time to teach a men's class in Sunday school. We would be happy to have you attend with us, but only if you want to. It is not a requirement for your position here. Laila usually goes her own way on Sunday, and we do not feel we can dictate to her."

Again Katie was swept by the certainty that currents eddied through the house that were not evident in the surface relationships.

Later, lying stretched out in bed with the curtains open to the brilliance of the moonless, star-filled sky, Katie thought back over the conversation. She remembered the unexplained stops, the several times Mrs. Sieverson's words had seemed to go off in a strange direction. She had made a point of the fact that Andrew was a bank examiner, whatever that was, as though it should mean something to her. And was there some significance in Andrew's saying, "We really want to help you" or in Mrs. Sieverson's, "No matter what, I believe you are a loving person"?

Katie half smiled. What a marvelous plot this would make for a mystery story—providing it had a happy ending with no dark shadows to complicate it. Actually, there was absolutely no reason she should not stop being suspicious of every look and word and simply enjoy being here. After all, she was not a prisoner. Mrs. Sieverson had given her a key. She could pack her suitcases and walk out the front door anytime she wanted to—right now if she wanted to.

She felt herself gradually relaxing on the clean, fragrant sheets. The soft night sounds made her drowsy. Then she came wide awake and, on impulse, got up and crossed the soft blue carpet, and turned the lock under the hand-painted china doorknob.

FOUR

Katie awoke the next morning to the quiet unfamiliarity of the house. She had left the curtains and windows open to the fresh, cool air, and now the warm sun poured into the room, highlighting the soft blue enamel on the furniture and reflecting the glow of the pale yellow walls. The chirp of birds in the trees beyond the windows was the only sound to lift the deep silence of the house. In the bright daylight, the fingers of fear that had touched her last night and made her lock the door seemed foolish. How could she really imagine that this elegant, wealthy, respected home held currents of intrigue and dark shadows?

She lay there, her mind still drowsy, thinking of Mrs. Sieverson. Her charm and gaiety could not possibly be a cover for something sinister. The thought was ridiculous.

And her nephew? Katie thought about Andrew, wondering how old he was. Surely not yet thirty. She remembered her first sight of him, his lean angular face and easy posture, his movements that were

57

quick and yet unhurried, and the way his smile came slowly to light his serious face with a steady, warm glow that spread to his lips and was reflected into his eyes, deepening the blue. But that was not true when he looked directly at her now. His expression was no longer warm and friendly as it had been at their first meeting. Instead, his eyes and face were guarded, questioning, with a cold look that shut her out and made her feel awkward and guilty.

She threw back the sheet with sudden decision and got up. "Imagination again." She said the words out loud to make them seem more reassuring and went in to shower.

As she dressed in the quiet charm of the room, a clock chimed melodiously downstairs. Katie remembered with regret the noise and lack of hot water and the lukewarm, faucet-made coffee that Jane was still enduring. She looked at her reflection in the mirror as she tied a bright orange scarf around the neck of her beige sweater, and her hands were momentarily stilled. She wondered again, uneasily, by what stroke of luck she had been rescued from the drabness of Mrs. Ireland's rooming house to the light graciousness of this place. She had been rescued not only from a dreary place, but also from the fear that she might not be able to manage financially. Now this gift of room and board with a small salary and the little she had in the bank would easily take her through the year.

She tied the scarf in a loose knot and shook herself from worry. "Just accept your good luck," she scolded herself sternly.

Her footsteps were lost in the thick carpeting as she went down the stairs and felt the silence of the house follow her into the living room. The draperies on the far side of the room were partially open to the morning sun. The glimpse she had from across the room of the white sails of several boats dipping in the gentle swell of the waves, pulled her to the window. The sun reflected on the water, giving the appearance of sparkling diamonds shimmering in blue and gold sparks of light. In broad daylight, the tangle of bushes and rocks and stunted trees that lined the cliff below the window did not look as ominous as they had the day before.

As she watched, a larger boat came slowly into view. The bridge opened deliberately before it. She moved closer to the window to see it better, knowing that not many weeks remained for boats to transport cargo before ice closed the lake in for the long winter. As she pulled the draperies wider to watch the ship's slow, stately progress, her eyes caught a movement as though someone were slipping along the edge of the sheer cliff that dropped to the rocks and waves below. She caught her breath, wanting instinctively to call out a warning to be careful not to plunge over the precipice. She watched, standing half-hidden in the heavy gold curtains, her hand to her mouth in alarm. Something flashed sharply up toward the house, and she stared at the quick gleam. It flashed again, and then again.

Like a signal, something inside her whispered. But of course that was silly. There was nothing out there because there was no safe way anyone could possibly be out in the dense underbrush so near the sheer drop.

As she stood by the window, puzzled by the flash of light, she felt her aloneness in the silent house, and an unreasoning fear made her turn and hurry into the dining room. The table was set for dinner with a lace-edged linen tablecloth, monogrammed heavy silver, and the icy brilliance of crystal goblets. A graceful, sloping, cut-glass bowl filled with orange and gold flowers splashed color in the center of the table.

She pushed open the swinging louvered doors into the kitchen and found a note propped against a rooster sugar bowl.

"Katie, we've gone to church. Help yourself to breakfast. Back by 12:30."

The clock over the refrigerator said 11:45. Dinner was apparently cooking slowly in the oven, and she did not know what else to do toward preparing it, so she took a cinnamon roll from the covered plate on the table and wandered out to see what the back of the house was like.

She discovered there was no back yard because the house was built too near the edge of the cliff. Instead the door opened from the kitchen onto a narrow porch. A door at one end of the porch took her out to a wide expanse of carefully clipped lawn circled by a deep, curving bank of flowers. A low, foot-wide stone wall that came just below her waist securely bordered the far side of the flower bed. The wall ran the length of the Sieverson property as far as she could see and apparently continued on to the property next door.

To satisfy her curiosity that there was no safe way up or down the cliff, she stepped across the flower bed to lean over the wall. She felt the rough stones pressing against her legs through the thin cotton skirt and saw only a dizzying drop of hillside falling in sheer rock to other jagged rocks below. She had no idea how far it was down to the shore. Whoever had built this house had in mind protection against attacking enemies coming across the water.

She smiled at her imagination. That's what came from reading countless stories of kings and castles and moats and dungeons. Who could imagine enemies in the quiet peace of this exclusive part of town?

Katie took a wide step back across the flowers and strolled along the still-green grass, stopping to pick a vivid zinnia. As she walked, she looked up at the red-gabled roof of the big house and remembered a snatch of something she had read about Swedish people's liking red houses. This one was white, but the roof was a deep barn red.

She looked around for neighbors. The nearest house was barely discernible behind a beautiful stand of spruce and evergreen trees on the far side of the lawn. It too was white with a red roof. Swedes again? That would be logical in this north country. From where she stood, the only other visible part of the house was a row of windows along the top just under the roof. They were all heavily shuttered, giving it a closed up, deserted look. It was the only house within sight on this side of the street. If there were some on the other side, they were hidden behind trees and shrubbery. It was a lonely spot. Again she found herself imagining the original builder looking for space, not wanting to be hemmed in.

Like Daniel Boone, feeling crowded when a few thousand people moved into his state.

Her curiosity about the Sieverson family was growing. What a fascinating history must be behind them. She strolled along the wide driveway to the entrance and looked up at the graceful lines of the ships that were carved on the posts. They were so finely done one could see them leaning hard into the stiffly blowing breeze, making for port before the storm's fury broke around them.

Dad would have been intrigued by them.

The thought brought his memory into sharp, aching focus. She stood in the hot, autumn sunshine in the unfamiliarity of someone else's house, lost and alone and deserted.

Then a car, a sleek, red convertible, turned the corner at the end of the street and came slowly along. It stopped opposite her, its motor purring softly. The driver leaned across the front seat and smiled up at her.

"Are you just out walking in this end of town or are you visiting the Sieversons?"

Katie hesitated; her natural reserve shrouded her. But his contagious smile that crinkled the tanned skin beside his eyes and emphasized the friendliness of his face made her return the smile.

"Are you a neighbor?"

He nodded toward the next house. "I belong to the

old Jorgenson homestead." He looked back at her, frankly admiring. "And I've been in and out of this house often enough and eaten Aunt Sieverson's bread and jam and cookies long enough to know that you've not been here before."

As Katie hesitated, wondering how to explain, he added, "I'll bet you're another one of her stray kittens."

She did not answer his words because the smile that went with them and the light blue eyes laughing up at her suddenly jogged her memory, and she studied his face, frowning.

He laughed at her scrutiny. "You're trying to remember where you've seen me before."

She nodded.

He sat with one arm flung along the top of the seat and said, "I'm your library science fiction fan."

"Of course! But—you—you look different."

"Oh, I probably still had my mustache that day." He rubbed his clean-shaven upper lip. "And I may have had on my glasses. I need them to read. Let's see— that was last week? Yeah, I've been to the barber since then to get rid of what my mother calls my shaggy dog look. She thinks it looks sloppy. I give in to her now and then."

Katie leaned her elbows on the edge of the rolled-down window and smiled back at him. "I'm not working there anymore, so someone else will have to supervise your reading."

"Listen, I've been going to that library since I was a kid, so I've about read it out. I can't count the times Miss Elder has bawled me out for forgetting to wipe my feet on the mats she puts out on rainy days."

He grinned at her. "She didn't see me the other day or she would have bawled me out for getting fresh with the pretty librarian." He settled himself more comfortably and asked, "So how come you are here?"

"You said I was one of Mrs. Sieverson's stray kittens," she challenged him.

"Hey, look, I'm sorry. I didn't mean that the way it sounded. It's just that I know Mrs. Sieverson. You couldn't find a kinder, gentler person. She's always doing something for someone and never asks for anything in return."

He looked at her intently. His eyes narrowed, hardening the expression on his face. "You couldn't have gotten a better deal."

Katie straightened and drew back. "It is not a deal," she snapped. "I've been hired. I'm going to earn my room and board helping her with correspondence and some other things, some writing perhaps."

His expression changed swiftly again and warmed as he protested, "I'm sorry again! I didn't mean to imply that you were taking advantage of her. It's just that Mrs. Sieverson is such a—" He stopped, an appeal for understanding clear in his eyes. "My mother has been an invalid for years, so Mrs. Sieverson has been like a mother to me, and I feel very protective toward her."

He looked up at her, his expression teasing. "And after all, I don't know you. Remember, you didn't let me see what was in your purse, so I couldn't tell what kind of person you are."

His smile was disarming as he added, "But I'd like to know you better. Let's start all over again and get properly introduced."

He shut off the motor and got out of the car, came around to her, and leaned back against the car with his arms folded.

"I am Barry Jorgenson, college grad, in advertising with my father, frustrated potential Olympic swimmer, basically lazy, independently wealthy— whatever that really means—unmarried but looking."

"So you've known the Sieversons a long time?" She felt oddly reassured that he could vouch for them. Though she scarcely knew him, she felt she could trust him, especially since he was a neighbor.

"All my life. My folks have always lived next door. Lars and I hiked to school and swam and skated together—"

"Lars?"

"Mrs. Sieverson's only son." He looked at her intently, and then shook his head, his eyes sober. "I don't suppose she has spoken of him to you yet. She will sometime soon, because she considers him to still be alive."

"You mean he's missing? Not in the war—?"

Barry shook his head. "No, he is dead. He went through thin ice on the lake while skating when he was a kid. No one could get to him in time. His numbed fingers slipped from the edge of the ice he was trying to hang onto." His voice was somber as he stared off across the driveway. Listening, Katie shivered, rubbing her bare arms, which felt cold in spite of the sun's warmth.

"But what makes her think he is still alive? She isn't into—she's not mixed up in some occult group?" Katie asked in sudden alarm.

He gave an abrupt, explosive laugh. "No! At least, not in the way you're thinking. But she does have this strong, unshakeable belief in life after death. I mean, real life in a definite place. And so does Andy." He looked down at her. "You've met Andrew, of course."

She nodded.

"Good, steady, dependable Andrew." His tone was slightly mocking, and she looked at him questioningly.

"Now don't get me wrong. I like old Andy. But he *is* a stodgy old guy."

Katie felt quick, unreasoning resentment flare. She had no particular reason to like Andrew, but Barry's picture did not seem accurate or fair.

She listened as Barry went on. "He's a couple of years older than Lars and I. Let's see—we were in the sixth grade when it happened; Andy was in his first year of high school. Not that he was that much older. He had skipped a grade in school. He's a brain, no question about that. Because he was older he usually bossed us around, though Lars never minded."

He stopped, looking off across the grass, his eyes shrouded and his jaw muscles tense. Katie sensed he was back in thought to that terrible accident. Then he roused and shrugged, and his voice was once again light and teasing as he said, "You've still not told me your name. With those big, dark eyes and dark hair, I wouldn't guess you were Miss Scandinavia."

66

"I'm Katie Cameron, new at the university, working on a master's degree in history. Mrs. Sieverson invited me to live here for the year. I just came yesterday."

"Yesterday? So you didn't know about this the day we talked?"

She shook her head. "Actually it was that same day we talked, later in the evening, that they came in and offered me the job."

"How did they happen to pick you?" His voice showed his interest.

"I don't know. But it's unbelievably good luck for me."

She did not realize that her voice carried a plea for understanding and reassurance until Barry nodded back at her, his smile flashing again. "That's just the kind of thing Aunt Sieverson always does. That's why I made that reference to stray kittens. She likes people, and she likes to help whenever she can. And you're the one she found this time."

His admiration for Mrs. Sieverson rang so deep and genuine in his voice that Katie felt the remnants of anxiety begin to dissolve. But she was jolted by the swift change in his tone when he added, "We can't forget Laila in all this." He studied her face. "You've met her?"

"Yes, just briefly. Last night at dinner."

"But not heard her story?"

"No."

"You should. But don't ask her."

He looked beyond her down the street and straightened up. With a slow, easy stride he walked around and got in the car and lifted his hand in a wave. "I'll see you again sometime, Katie Cameron."

She watched his car take off up the street out of sight and then turned at the sound of another car coming along the street and slowing to turn into the driveway between the two graceful, welcoming ships. Mrs. Sieverson waved from where she sat in the front seat beside Andrew, and Katie felt quick pleasure that Laila was not with them. She had wondered last evening, listening to the dinner table conversation, if Laila and Andrew dated. Her admiring look at him had been obvious. His attitude toward her had been inclusive and friendly, with no doubt or suspicion showing.

She followed the car along the driveway, thinking about Barry and the glimpses he had given of the family. He was fun. Both times they had met he had kept her laughing. Most of all he had convinced her that there was nothing sinister in the invitation to live here.

Watching Mrs. Sieverson get out of the car, Katie wondered why she had needed such reassurance. Mrs. Sieverson's smile as she waited for Katie to reach her, and the unmistakeable sincerity of her voice as she asked, "Did you sleep well?" were so genuine they swept away the last of the dark suspicions she had been harboring.

As long as she did not look at Andrew and see his reservations about her, she could believe that this was going to be a good year, a year filled with the trust and companionship she had known with her parents.

68

FIVE

A contented, at-home feeling deepened as the week went by, and Katie settled into a comfortably easy routine. At the beginning of the semester she had worked out a schedule that left her free to work afternoons and evenings and all day Saturday at the library. With Mrs. Sieverson only requiring her help a few hours each afternoon to answer correspondence, Katie felt a relaxing freedom. And even those hours were easy and interesting, made so partly by Mrs. Sieverson's sharing of herself.

Afternoon coffee, served from the antique silver coffee service into a variety of delicate china cups, became a much anticipated ritual. Mrs. Sieverson insisted on Katie's unwinding from her day of classes before starting work.

"Not having gone to college myself, I try to learn all I can from others," she confided. "History has always fascinated me. Not so much places, for I have not cared so much to travel. But people—people and the things that happened to them is what makes history."

"But you travel all over the world by letter." Katie riffled through the envelopes with stamps from Africa, Alaska, Japan, Peru, and the Phillippines. "You have so many friends."

"Some of them are only friends-by-mail; I have not met them yet. But even they are as real to me as my friends here in town."

After a moment she said, "Katie, I would like us to be a team on this. I will dictate answers to the letters—"

"But I told you that I don't type at all well," Katie protested. "I mean, not well enough to take dictation. And my shorthand is just my own abbreviated style."

"Let me see a sample of it, may I?"

"What shall I say? May I take something out of one of the letters?"

Mrs. Sieverson handed her one. She read it through quickly and copied the last paragraph in several lines of her scribble.

Mrs. Sieverson looked at it and shook her head, laughing. "What *does* this say?"

Katie translated. " 'Behold, as the eyes of servants look unto the hand of their masters, and as the eyes of a maiden unto the hand of her mistress; so our eyes wait upon the Lord our God, until that he have mercy upon us.' Psalm 123:2." As she repeated the words, she realized that they made hardly more sense to her than the shorthand symbols did to Mrs. Sieverson.

"You do have your own system! May I show this to Andrew?"

"Y-yes. I—guess so."

70

She answered reluctantly, hating the thought of his laughing at the funny-looking marks and thinking worse of her than he already did. She made an involuntary movement to take the paper back. But Mrs. Sieverson had folded it in half and sat absently creasing the folded edge as she went on explaining her plans.

"You need not be an expert typist to help me, Katie. You see, my answers to these letters really should be personally written. But I have arthritis in my hands which makes it difficult for me to write very long at a time. Perhaps together we can work out a general letter giving some paragraphs of news and information you can type. Then I can personalize each one by adding a few lines to each by hand. These friends need encouraging letters, and I would like to try writing them this way."

Most of the letters came from and went to missionaries, people as remote to Katie as though they were from another planet. But to Mrs. Sieverson, each one was a close friend, whose children she knew by name and whose work and its problems she gave her individual attention.

Reading the letters day after day, Katie found her mind saturated with phrases from them, quaint expressions that were hauntingly beautiful. Someone spoke of being "shadowed with wings," and another of being fastened "as a nail in a sure place." Then she discovered that the expressions usually were from the Bible. The people who wrote the letters were Mrs. Sieverson's interest; it was the words they used that

71

fascinated Katie and began to open another world to her.

She worked with Mrs. Sieverson in the comfortable study off the dining room. It was a businesslike room with filing cabinets and a massive desk. A large world map stretched across one wall, punctuated with miniature flags of the countries where her friends lived and worked. The small-paned windows on the far side of the room opposite the door looked out on the side lawn, each window pane framing a different picture. One showed an expanse of carefully trimmed and edged grass, another a single stately evergreen, still another a blaze of colored leaves on the huge oak tree that stood like a sentinel in the middle of the side lawn. Beyond the grove of trees at the far edge of the lawn and barely seen from the windows, was the house Barry belonged to. Whenever Katie looked out at it, it had the same remote, deserted appearance it seemed to have with her first glimpse of it. She could not imagine Barry with his quicksilver wit and personality belonging to it. *It must be a reflection of his invalid mother,* she thought idly, and wondered if they would ever meet, and whether Mrs. Sieverson ever visited her.

Intriguing as that house was, this one was even more so. Katie was curious about Mrs. Sieverson's careful locking of the files and desk at the end of each day and watched her.

Mrs. Sieverson saw the question in her eyes and explained. "This shows what childhood influence can do. As a child I followed my grandfather around his house—not at all like this one—while he carefully

72

locked everything, doors, windows, anything that could be locked or bolted. He did not do it for protection from burglars; he had nothing of value. But he brought with him from the old country a terrible, oppressive fear of the unknown. To him, locked doors were a barrier to unwanted spirits. It was a burdensome fear. His parents brought it with them and they fit in with the Indians around them and their belief in spirits. The fear was needless, of course, but as a child I did not know that, and I was impressed with his seriousness. Now I lock because I have learned it is simply a sensible precaution."

"I'd like to know more about the people who first came and settled here," Katie said shyly. "As you know history is my major, and Dad taught history. He and Mother read a lot to me, and one of my favorite subjects was the pioneers. But they've never been really *people* to me, never really lived. Now, knowing something of the Sieversons and your ancestors makes them seem more alive."

"I don't think you or I in our comfortable situation can begin to imagine the incredible bravery of those early settlers," Mrs. Sieverson said slowly, her voice thoughtful. "It took a special kind of courage for them to leave their homes and go out into the unknown. I particularly admire those who came north to settle this part of the country, my ancestors among them. Those original settlers came to Indians and grasshoppers and cold and loneliness."

Her words slowed and stopped altogether. Katie sat in the silence, watching Mrs. Sieverson retreat into the past, absorbed by the harshness of the life that seemed so vivid to her. Then she brightened as she went on with the story.

"This state has an intensely interesting history. From its beginning it made an enormous contribution to the wealth and stability of the country. And it played an active part in trying to keep the nation from being torn apart by civil war. It was the first state in the union to volunteer soldiers to the Union army. Its soldiers, some of them mere boys, were the turning point in the Gettysburg victory—if that battle can be called a victory. Three Sieverson men were lost in the carnage at Bull Run, nameless even on the casualty lists. A great deal of history lies wrapped in the walls and roof of this house when you think of the people it has sheltered—both good and bad. That is true also of other families whose roots are buried deep in the north country."

Her voice showed strain as she finished the sentence. Her manner was tense underneath an outward calm. Then she shook off the mood and focused her eyes again on Katie.

"This is an exposed area of the shore, as you have probably noticed. Any building would take the brunt of the weather, so the house was built very sturdy to stand the storms off the lake. They took down some trees to clear the land and give a view to the lake, but they left as many as possible. The first Sieversons seemed to crave the sound of waves crashing on the rocks in order to feel at home. That is why they chose this isolated spot to build instead of selecting a more sheltered area."

"But why didn't they put the house farther back

from the cliff? Whenever I look out I'm reminded of castles that need protection from enemies."

Mrs. Sieverson nodded at that. Her expression was serious. "It was designed with the need for protection in mind. You see, the settlers who came here originally were not the way the books often picture immigrants, poor souls who came fleeing from oppression by government. Many of those were so beaten by life already that they simply huddled in big cities and somehow existed.

"But the first immigrants to this part of the country were fiercely independent. They came, many of them, from comfortable backgrounds that had become too comfortable and were stifling their sense of adventure. That was not true of all of them, of course, but it was certainly true of the Sieversons. The first Andrew was big, strong, independent—and not a good man. In other circumstances he might easily have been a pirate. Some people thought one of his sons was, finding and keeping belongings from ships that broke up in some of the terrible lake storms. When fog closed in, ships could easily be battered on the rocks below the house."

Katie sat listening in the stillness of the room, which was a frame for the picture that Mrs. Sieverson's gentle voice unfolded. A picture of people crossing wild seas, helpless at times in the waves that washed the decks, and surviving on rotten, moldy food. Then they had to endure the numbing cold of winter in a crude cabin while a house went up slowly, the loneliness of the silent forest without neighbors, the death of two little children the first year, crop failure.

"And Indian attacks were a constant threat. There were missionaries, brave souls, who worked among the Indians, the Sioux especially. But treaties were not honored by the government and hate resulted, directed at the settlers who were taking over the land. A terrible Sioux uprising in 1862, one of the bloodiest in the history of the country, took many of the new state's citizens and frightened away others who planned to settle the land. Only the brave stayed—or the foolish, depending on your point of view. The Sieversons were among those who stayed."

"And your ancestors?"

Mrs. Sieverson shook her head. Her voice was reluctant. "No. My people were later coming. They came from a lower class structure in the old country and were a long time freeing themselves from that bondage."

The words came as a shock to Katie. Where then had she acquired that air of poise and mastery? Sitting as she always did, her shoulders gracefully straight, her slender back not touching the chair, she seemed taller than she was and very much in command. Katie studied her. She had not only an outward but an inner control as well, an inner strength.

She realized that Mrs. Sieverson had resumed the story and was saying, "The settlers faced not only Indian attacks, but invasions from grasshoppers that ate crops to the bare, brown earth. Since you know history, you have heard this story before, and perhaps you have thought it sheer exaggeration. But I know it is true because I have a diary with a heartbreaking note by one little wife who tells how she carefully tended her garden during the spring and early summer, protecting every tender green shoot. One summer day she went into the house for a pan to hold the lettuce and peas she was going to pick for the noon meal. She heard a loud whirring noise, and in the moment it took to hurry outside, the garden was gone, stripped by grasshoppers. Not a bit of green was left."

Katie shivered after the telling. "I'm afraid the country never would have been settled if everyone were like me. I don't have a strong spirit of adventure. Not that strong at least."

"Neither did all those wives, certainly not the first Mrs. Sieverson. She was terribly young, with two babies and, according to her diary, a consuming fear of the unknown. But, of course, she had no other choice but to follow her husband."

"I'm glad women don't have to do it that way anymore." Katie looked across at her employer, expecting a shocked reply, and was surprised to see laughter in her eyes.

"You've never been in love, Katie."

"I don't think love has to include blindly following whatever notion the other person gets."

"Sometimes a woman has no other choice. I have often thought of that young wife since I read her diary many years ago now. She 'blindly' trusted herself to a man whose eyes saw only adventure in a new land, never the hardships. Did she feel cheated? I don't know; she never said. Perhaps we women need more of that kind of trust."

"Did she ever regret that she had no choice?" Katie challenged. "You said that first Sieverson was not a good man. Didn't she ever stand up to him? Express her own ideas? Decide what was best for herself and the children those times he was wrong?"

"Ah, Katie, it is so easy to judge other people when we look back on them, especially when we stand on the fringe of another generation. I cannot do that. All the Sieversons owe a great deal to that little wife. The family history is a rich one—as I am sure yours is also." She smiled at Katie, taking any sting of rebuke from her words.

"You mentioned a diary. Are there other diaries or letters or records from those early years?"

"Yes, I have a few treasured things," Mrs. Sieverson answered with what Katie thought was deliberate vagueness. Then she said, "I am sure you have noticed that my missionary friends have exactly the same kind of trust we have been talking about. They go out into the unknown too. The difference is that their trust is in God, who is completely dependable. It is not blind trust in someone who might be wrongly motivated or have mistaken judgment. They have a settled conviction that God is personally leading them. They have an all-or-nothing way of life in their commitment to God."

She reached for a letter. "Do you remember the promise the Jordans said they were relying on when they went to work in the eye hospital in Africa?" She quoted softly, " 'I will bring the blind by a way that they knew not; I will lead them in paths that they have not known: I will make darkness light before them, and crooked things straight. These things will I do unto them, and not forsake them.' "*

Katie looked back at her thoughtfully. "That means they have to believe that God actually exists."

"You are saying you do not?"

"I—I don't know. To be honest, I have never thought about Him the way you do, as though He were real."

"He is as real to me as you are."

"How can He be? I'm a person—I'm alive."

"So is God. Katie, I am not talking about what some people mean when they refer to God as though He were some sort of idea man has created, or a good influence that surrounds us. There is only one God, the One who is the God and Father of the Lord Jesus Christ. Any other concept of Him, no matter how sincere or lofty or reverent, that leaves out this fact is false."

Katie struggled to be polite and yet make clear her objection to such a sweeping claim.

"That's a very narrow idea, isn't it? It strikes out all the good that there is in other religions."

"You will think me very dogmatic, I know, when I say that as a college graduate you have been exposed to all the philosophical nonsense about there being many ways to heaven. There is no truth whatever to the poetic idea that God accepts 'Turk and Brahmin' because they reached Him through their

*Isaiah 42:16

79

gods. God's invitation to men is inclusive—it is for all men. But the *way* to God is exclusive. It is a narrow way, through Jesus Christ alone."

"And those who can't come that way because they have never heard of Him?"

"That is why my missionary friends leave all and go across the world to find such people," Mrs. Sieverson answered simply. She shook her head. "Oh, Katie, I cannot give you an adequate answer to that question. I can only trust God in that as in everything. Dare we think we are more loving, more caring than He is?"

Katie looked across at Mrs. Sieverson's confident face. The memory of Barry's somber story about Lars echoed in her ears, and she looked compassionately at the gentle woman opposite her. The tragedy obviously had driven her to this need to cling to something outside herself. It had in time become a fixed habit and now was the force around which her life revolved. It showed in her intimate relationship with missionaries who otherwise were strangers, in the hour she spent each morning reading her Bible, in the mottoes like the one in the old-fashioned frame over the kitchen sink with the words *God is love* carefully worked in blue and yellow crossstitching. Katie felt a rush of affection mixed with pity.

However this habit had originated, it obviously satisfied some deep psychological need. It was like other customs she followed so religiously.

Like her weekly baking of cinnamon rolls and bread, Katie thought. Each Saturday, pans lined the scrubbed-white center kitchen table, their lightly browned, rounded tops sending out spice and sugar fragrance as they cooled. Years of such baking had built a habit that continued long beyond need. One was a physical habit; the other, a spiritual.

But Katie frowned to herself over another thought. She could understand Mrs. Sieverson's strong belief in God, but what caused it for Andrew? Though she had been with them only ten days, it was clear they both lived with God. Andrew also read his Bible daily, talked naturally about God, went to church because he wanted to. Could a practical, hard-headed, modern businessman be taken in by religion? Especially as suspicious a person as Andrew seemed to be?

But maybe he was only suspicious about her. And again the question nagged—*why?*

She was aware then that Mrs. Sieverson sat watching her. The expression in her eyes revealed her inner thoughts. An unspoken question was there that Katie could plainly read. *What about you, my dear?*

She shifted restlessly, and to change the subject asked abruptly, "And the house next door, the Jorgensons. When was that built?"

She saw Mrs. Sieverson's fingers tighten on the coffee cup she held. After a moment she put it down carefully, staring down at it. When she finally spoke, her voice was controlled and even, almost colorless.

"The Jorgenson house went up several years after this one. The two families, that is, the original families, came over on the ship together and became close friends. They came to this state together, both wanting climate and surroundings similar to what they had grown up in. But the Sieversons came

81

straight here to what then was a tiny, isolated settlement clinging to the hillside along the lake, while the Jorgensons stopped with other friends farther south. After a time they came on here and have been here ever since. They and others—immigrants if you will—gradually changed the land from raw, wild frontier to settled, secure farms. Both families have been a part of the city's growth in lumbering, mining, shipping. There were times they lived only on potatoes, turnips, and cabbage while they struggled to clear the land. People depended on one another, they needed one another then just to survive. The two families have always been friends, living here side by side overlooking the lake."

She looked then at Katie with a questioning frown. "You know who lives there?"

"Yes. I first met Barry in the library—well, the day I met you actually. And then that first Sunday morning while you were in church, he drove by while I was outside. He recognized me and stopped, surprised to see me here. I asked where he lived and he said he was your neighbor and that his mother was an invalid."

"Yes. She has not been out of the house for many years."

Her voice was bleak and forlorn, and Katie sensed she was back in memory to other scenes. She heard Barry's words, "Lars, her only son, lost."

The awfulness of the scene stood before her as vividly as if she were actually seeing it. The sound of the cracking ice ringing like shots across the cold stillness of the lake and echoing up to the house on the cliff; Lars's desperate call for help as his numbed fingers gradually weakened their grasp at the ragged edge of the ice; the dark water spreading over the surface, soaking into his heavy clothing and dragging him under. To have watched and heard the despairing, "Mother, help me!" and not be able to help. To see the beloved head slip under the ice and be lost forever—

"Katie?"

With an effort she wrenched her thoughts back, remembering that it was Mrs. Sieverson and not she who had gone through the terrible experience. She felt tears clinging to her eyelashes as she smiled tremulously at Mrs. Sieverson's concerned face and anxious eyes.

"Your two families must have shared experiences that are too personal to put down for anyone to see."

Mrs. Sieverson nodded, a bright smile fixed on her lips. Her fingers trembled and she clasped her hands tightly together on the glass top of the big desk. Her eyes were wide and darkly blue as she looked beyond Katie into the past.

"Yes," she said. "We have many memories."

SIX

Katie found herself looking forward to the hours spent in the small study and the interesting collage of time that seemed to be there. On the one hand was the look into the future in the confident letters that came and went all over the world. On the other, was the sense of history coming to life in Mrs. Sieverson's reminiscing. She began to feel that she too had lived with these people who felt at home along the lake where water constantly pounded the rocks, and wind sometimes shrieked, sometimes sifted soothingly through the tops of the trees.

As they worked together one gray day with rain whispering outside the windows in quiet, shushing sounds, Mrs. Sieverson said, "Katie, you have such a way with words, have you ever thought of writing?"

"No, not really. I think I love words because I read constantly as a child. And was read to. My earliest memories are of sitting with my mother's arm around me while she read aloud books that I'm sure were not on a child's recommended reading list. I cried over *Black Beauty* before I was old enough to understand it. I only sensed the sadness the words held. Words have so much power. They have so many subtle shades of meaning. That's where I part company with the current crop of high school kids and even my college friends who have such a limited vocabulary. When I did my college student teaching with seniors in high school, I was appalled at the insensitivity most young people have to words."

She stopped and gestured in apology. "I'm sorry, I didn't mean to lecture." Then she added, "That's why I'm so much enjoying this work. Because of the letters, I mean, and the pictures they bring of—of different kinds of people."

She stopped herself abruptly, not wanting to admit the effect the words were having on her. There were the ones she had just read, for example, from a couple who had been forced to leave a village because of opposition—"The harvest is past, the summer is ended, and they are not saved." The poignancy of the words gripped her. But it was only because the thought fit the pictures Mrs. Sieverson had painted of those early settlers. She would *not* let the words be more personal.

Mrs. Sieverson sat idly turning the little silver-handled paper knife she used so carefully to open each letter.

"You *are* just the person I need, Katie. For a long time I have thought of gathering material in order to leave a permanent record of the Sieverson family." She stopped and gave a quick laugh. "I almost said *my* family. I have belonged to it so long one way or another that I think of it that way. Working up a family history is just a personal whim with me, and perhaps no one else will be interested in it, but Andrew is the last of the Sieverson name, and it does seem too bad for what once was a large, vigorous, influential family to disappear with no remembrance. And Andrew does not seem to be doing anything to insure that the family name will continue."

"He's not interested in anyone special?" Katie kept her voice light, her tone casual.

"No. He dated a good bit during high school and college, but on a friendly, not romantic, basis. Then after college, two intense years spent in graduate study did not give time to build the kind of friendships that lead to marriage. Perhaps this year will change that. I would never presume to interfere with Andrew on this, because of course he has his own ideas."

The words were said matter-of-factly, but Katie wondered if Mrs. Sieverson was letting her know in a kind way that there was no use in her becoming interested in him. If so, it was an unnecessary warning, since he obviously had no intention of building a friendship with her. She found the thought edged with regret.

Mrs. Sieverson had not expected an answer, for she went on, "I have enough pieces of information that could be written up in a connected way to make a history of the Sieversons—just for the family, of course, not for publication. But I have needed someone who could put it all together with just the right words. Will you help me do it?"

"I'd like to!" Katie heard the eagerness in her voice.

"Fine. Perhaps we can make some definite plans today. But first, shall we have coffee?" She filled two delicate cups and handed one to Katie. "Have I ever shown you how a Swede, a really old-time Swede, enjoys his coffee?"

When Katie shook her head, Mrs. Sieverson poured coffee into the saucer, put a lump of sugar in her mouth, and sipped the coffee slowly through it. "The art is to make the coffee and the sugar lump come out even," she said. Then she laughed at Katie over the saucer rim. "I can see your thoughts on your expressive face," she teased. "You are thinking what a contrast it is to drink coffee out of tissue-thin china but to do it like a peasant woman in a farmhouse."

"Well—I—I've—just never seen it done," Katie stammered, feeling her cheeks grow warm with embarrassment.

"It is not the most correct of manners. But it is an old custom, and it brings back memories."

She put down the coffee cup and said briskly, "Now let me show you some of the material."

She crossed the room and closed the study door. Then she came back and sat down in the big gold-brocade wing chair, patting the fat, low hassock beside her. "Come sit here with me. I want to show you some of these memories. They are treasures for their sentimental value only, not for any other reason."

She bent over and unlocked the door of the small wooden chest that stood beneath the window overlooking the side lawn. Reaching in to the top shelf, she pulled out a slim packet of letters, and nodded her reply when Katie exclaimed, "I think I know what hose are!"

"Yes. These are my—our—love letters. Not many, as you can see. My husband and I went to school together, and we were seldom apart during our married life so there was not a need to write. Then too, my husband died not many years after we were married."

"I'm sorry." But Katie sensed that the sadness in the words were for a fact long ago accepted. "Tell me how you met."

"Well, the Sieversons were a large family, and as I said they have always lived in this place since coming here originally. I think I told you once that Andrew's great-great-grandfather planned this house to celebrate the state's entrance into the union. Of course, it was only the bare beginning of what later became this spacious, beautiful home, but it was never just a crude log-cabin type either. That first Sieverson had been a craftsman in the old country, a cabinet-maker who built things to last, things of beauty. He passed this gift on to his sons and they to theirs, even to those who went into other lines of interests. They gradually built a reputation for fine work and with it a business. So they became one of the wealthier families very quickly and were one of the most respected and liked in the community. Respect and liking are not always deserved by the rich, you know. Too many acquire their wealth by walking over others. Of course, it was easier to get ahead in those days in this new, developing country that did not have

89

the class system most European countries did at
that time. The settlers left all that behind."

She stopped, thinking back. Katie saw the remote
expression in her eyes as she added, almost to herself, "But even here people were not always treated as
they should be, with equality and dignity."

She stopped again. Her expression, troubled, re-
gretful, showed her preoccupation with some un-
happy memory. Katie waited, not wanting to interrupt
the flow of memories by questions.

Mrs. Sieverson roused and went on. "But you were
asking how I met my husband. Even though there
were no real class distinctions, still there were differ-
ences. The city had the very rich and the very
poor—as it still does, of course. If you had seen my
home, you would be surprised that I ever got to know
the Sieversons. But it was this very lack of class
structure that was at least partly responsible. Inga
Sieverson and I were best friends in school. The
school district then covered a larger area than it does
now since the city has grown so much, so that even
though our homes were far apart, we went to the
same school. Inga was the ugly duckling of the family, though she became quite a handsome woman as
she matured and married. But as a child she was big
for her age, tall and gawky, with a too-big nose and
thin, fine, fly-away hair.

"I was a shy little person from an extremely poor
family living down by the railroad tracks. My father
worked on the docks, which was seasonal work of
course. When ice closed the lake to traffic, the men
were laid off until spring. Times were hard and my

father had very little education, so he could not find other jobs. That meant there was not money in the winter just when we needed it for warm coats and shoes. I felt the poverty keenly, conscious of my broken shoes and patched dresses. And children are cruel—" Her voice faltered a moment. "It is difficult to be so poor and be looked down on for that reason alone with no chance to prove one's worth."

Katie felt her throat tighten with pity as she watched Mrs. Sieverson turn the packet of letters over in her slender fingers as she went on. "So, both of us who stood on the edge of belonging, though for different reasons, became best friends. Inga was forever giving me the clothes she outgrew, even though they were much too big for me and my mother was not very good with a needle. Inga brought extra sandwiches for me in her lunch box, and I tagged after her in her outgrown, too-big-for-me overshoes." A smile turned the corners of her mouth, and she sat silent, immersed in the past.

"And so you married a brother," Katie finally prompted.

"Yes. A brother very much like Inga—tender, loving. We came here to live, and I have been here ever since. I stayed on when my husband died, because I had no other home. Gradually other family members moved away. Andrew's mother was never a strong person. Though his father, the only living son, inherited the house, they moved some years ago to a drier, warmer climate, and only come back to visit a few weeks each year. This is really Andrew's house now, but we share it. I don't know which one of us loves it more."

She leaned and pulled out a photograph album. "You'll see what I mean about how different Inga and I were."

Katie bent over the pictures, especially one of a fragile child with blond hair and bare feet. Her hand was tightly held by a tall, very plain, dark-haired girl, her hair tied severely back from her face in two long braids.

"How much older was she than you?"

"Just one year."

"She looks much older—and very protective of you."

"Yes, she was. She was my only real friend." Mrs. Sieverson looked down at the picture, running her fingertips lightly over it.

"The best thing she ever did for me was take me to Sunday school with her. My parents thought church was a lot of nonsense, but because her parents were rich, they let me go."

Mrs. Sieverson looked across at Katie and said simply, "My father drank, especially during the winter months when he had no work and too much time to think of the injustices of life. I did not know it then, did not understand that he did it from the desperation of seeing his children's faces as they watched other people's children with their Christmas trees and toys, and he was helpless to provide even our necessities. We only knew we had to hide from his anger that struck out at us. These are things we sometimes learn too late," she finished, her voice laced with sad regret.

Katie could find no words to answer the pathos coming through the simple telling of the story. But there had to be more to it. What could have changed the thin waif of a child in patched clothes into the confident, gracious woman opposite her?

She listened as Mrs. Sieverson's soft voice continued. "Inga insisted that her parents come down to our shack and get me every Sunday. Sometimes I stayed with her overnight on Saturday's—in the little room you are in. That is why I treasure the room, I suppose. It has such memories. But you see, that is how I came to know God, through the Sieversons. I owe Inga a great deal. My eternal security came to me because of her friendship."

Katie was deeply moved by the quiet words and felt rebuked. Her first assessment of what lay behind Mrs. Sieverson's faith had been too shallow. It was not just the loss of Lars; it was her whole history.

She looked down at the picture. "What became of her?"

The answer was so long in coming that she looked up to see Mrs. Sieverson's hands covering her face. Katie could see her lips pressed tightly together to stop their trembling. The words were a wisp of sound. "She—went away."

Katie wanted to ask if they ever wrote to each other, but she did not because Mrs. Sieverson's hurt was too plain. Maybe she meant Inga had died, and did not want to say so plainly.

She turned the pages of the album, her eyes

93

skimming the pictures. There were pages of happy family groups, of picnics along the lake, of posed portraits. There were school and graduation and wedding pictures. There were some of Mrs. Sieverson and Inga as young mothers. Then there were pages of baby and children's pictures. She tried not to linger too obviously over those of Andrew as a boy and later in cap and gown. Barry was there too in swim trunks, as a Boy Scout, and in a group with other boys. Katie wondered which one was Lars. Then the pictures ended abruptly in one album, and she turned over blank pages. Katie did not even look up with a question. None was necessary. There should have been pictures of a happy little boy named Lars in swim trunks, boy scout uniform, cap and gown. But there were none.

After a moment she said, "You're right. You do have material for a story." She laid the album down, shaken by sadness. She could not speak of Lars since his mother had not.

Mrs. Sieverson was reaching to take more letters and clippings from the little chest and said, her voice muffled, "I think we can arrange the family history from the beginning in a connected story. Both the history and the geography of this part of the country are tied in with the Sieverson family. And with other families who were equally important in settling this whole area."

"How far back do these letters and records go?"

"Just about the time of the Civil War, perhaps a year or two before. I have two letters from the family they left in Sweden, one written in such a tiny, spidery

94

script you will need a magnifying glass to read it. Then there is the slim little diary from the first Mrs. Sieverson, the one I mentioned earlier, which is heartbreaking to read. She writes of the separation from her mother—remember she was very young—and the strangeness of this area even though the climate and scenery were similar to what they had grown up with. She speaks of the children who died. I believe you will cry a little when you read it and be thankful you live in an easier day. Yet—I think you will catch her joy in following her husband and making a new life."

She smiled at Katie as she gathered up the packets of letters. Then she bent to grope to the back of the bottom shelf of the low chest, and took out a small green diary with a clasp lock. She sat looking at it, her hands tight on the covers. Her voice was thin and strained as she said, "I believe I will take all this upstairs to my bedroom."

"I'll help." Katie leaned to pick up the picture albums.

"Wait a minute, please." Mrs. Sieverson went over and opened the study door and looked out into the front hall. Katie watched her walk over to push open the swinging doors leading into the kitchen. Then she came back, picked up some of the material, and started up the stairs, beckoning to Katie.

When they reached the landing on the second floor, Mrs. Sieverson stopped and looked in through Laila's open bedroom door. Then she turned to Katie. "Wait here a moment while I put these away."

She took the albums Katie held, piling the letters

and diary on top of them, went into her room, and closed the door. When she came back a few minutes later, she apologized. "I know this seems very mysterious to you, and I am sorry. But if you do not know where I put these things, you will not need to be bothered keeping the secret."

Katie stood silent, not knowing what to answer. What idiosyncracy was this of Mrs. Sieverson? What could be so important in a bundle of old love letters and pictures of bygone days that they had to be hidden so secretly?

She listened then as Mrs. Sieverson went on, her voice low and troubled. "I do have a request to make that will seem strange to you. I can only say that I have a reason for asking it, a reason I would rather not explain just now. Will you promise not to let anyone know about the writing plans we have?"

She looked at Katie. Her expression made it clear that there was something she was not putting into words. She moistened her lips and repeated, "Please do not let Laila or—or anyone know what we are working on."

"Of course," Katie promised quickly. "But you don't know me—how do you know you can trust *me*?"

Mrs. Sieverson looked straight back at her. "Because I have come to know you in these two weeks. Your words, your actions, your appearance have revealed you more clearly than you realize."

"But you didn't know me when you offered me the job," Katie protested. "In fact—" She stopped, facing Mrs. Sieverson. This was the time to find out about the distrust she saw in Andrew's eyes and heard in the slightly formal way he spoke to her with a reserve that chilled his voice.

"Why *did* you invite me here? Andrew doesn't trust me at all, yet he went along with the job offer. Did he do it because you asked him to? And if so, why did you invite me when you knew nothing about me?"

"Katie, I will have to ask you simply to trust me. I am sure you will have all your questions answered some day—and so will we. I am confident there is an explanation for everything, my dear. As to why I insisted so on your coming—well, I told Andrew that you needed a shelter until the whole matter was worked out."

She patted Katie's arm affectionately and turned toward the stairs.

Katie stared after her wordlessly and leaned over the bannister to watch her go downstairs and into the kitchen to start dinner. What did she mean? Her answer only made the whole thing even more mysterious. What matter was she talking about? An explanation for what?

She had begun to feel at ease in the house and at the dinner table even when Andrew was home. But Mrs. Sieverson's strange remarks brought a rush of the uneasiness she had felt on first coming to the house. An inner constraint at dinner that evening made her stammer a confused, unclear answer when Andrew politely asked how she happened to choose this university for her graduate work. Her explanation came out sounding as though she were hiding something.

His noncommittal, "I see," plainly showed his disbelief.

The unreasonableness of his attitude infuriated her though she managed to keep a cool, aloof look under Laila's sly smile.

SEVEN

Anger still seethed the next day as she ate lunch with Jane, listening to her quick, light chatter.

"This is the first time we've really talked since you moved, Katie. I'm dying to hear all about it. Mark has a seminar this lunch hour, but he wants to know how things are going, too. Just wait until I tell him that you don't look quite so hollow-cheeked now. He'll insist it's because you're falling in love when actually it's because you are getting more to eat and are not working so hard."

Katie put her milk glass down with a thump and faced her. "Jane, there is absolutely *no* one out there to fall in love with! Andrew thinks I am out to gyp his aunt out of something. Suspicion leaps in his eyes every time he sees me. He can't stand me, and I feel the same way about him."

"Why would he be suspicious of you?" Jane objected. "*They* offered you the job, didn't they? You didn't ask them for it."

"I know. And don't ask me for an explanation of anything that goes on out there. I like Mrs. Sieverson.

99

I trust her. But nobody else in the house is even friendly. As for Barry—"

"Who's he?"

"A next-door neighbor. Really nice. But he's just the hail-fellow-well-met type. He's friendly, but he has no romance in mind whatever. He has lived all his life next door to the Sieversons in a big old gloomy-type house. I feel depressed whenever I see it. He calls Mrs. Sieverson 'Aunt,' which gives you some idea of what he's like. Charming, I guess some people would say."

"That's the kind you have to watch out for," Jane warned.

"Umm, not this one." Katie had a quick mental image of Barry's admiration of her as they stood by his car. But that had been two weeks ago and she had not seen him since.

She went on pouring out her frustrations. "And then there is Laila, whom I really can't figure out. She lives there too, but not in the same way I do. There's something there I can't put my finger on. From little things that are said now and then I get the feeling that she is connected somehow with the family in the past. I think she would love to marry the Sieverson money and position, but I don't believe Andrew is interested in her. Except as a person. I mean, I have to admit he is interested in *people*—like his aunt. He is very churchy like she is. But in a good sense," she added hastily. "Religion—church—God—faith— whatever you want to call it, really means something to them. It isn't fake."

Not wanting Jane to know how deeply Mrs. Sieverson's intimate friendship with God had begun to disturb her, Katie hurried on. "But for some reason, I am just a problem case of some kind. What kind and why I have no idea. When I ask why I was hired, I get some mysterious, evasive someday-you-will-understand answer. I may be moving back with you next semester after all—unless Andrew has me in jail first for some unexplained crime."

"Katie! That's terrible. You'd better move out right away before it gets more mysterious—or maybe even dangerous."

"I don't think there is any danger, physically I mean. But speaking of mysteries, Jane, I've got one here. I was going to show it to you before I moved out and kept forgetting it." She rummaged through her shoulder bag. "No, I left it home, I guess. It's several pages of funny-looking scribble I found in a book—"

"Listen to who's talking about funny looking scribble," Jane interrupted with a laugh. "Nothing's crazier than your shorthand, if you can call it that. Look, I've got to run to class. Put it in the mail and maybe Mark and I can figure it out. He's good at mysteries. And, hey, keep in touch. Don't let that place get you down."

"Anything you need returned to the downtown library? Mrs. Sieverson is at a luncheon, so I have some free time and have to look up some material."

"No, thanks. My lab experiments don't require too many books. Sorry I don't have time to walk with you; that's a long way."

I'd forgotten how far it is, Katie thought as she pulled open the heavy doors and stepped into the familiar room. Miss Elder was not at the desk to look at her over the tops of her glasses.

She browsed through the history section, turning pages of books while she leaned against the shelves. Groping for her notebook, she realized she had put her bag on a table and forgotten to pick it up as she moved farther along in the row. She hurried back, relieved to see it still on the table, and felt inside. The wallet was there with her money and identification intact, but the notebook was gone.

"I must have dropped it on the way in," she muttered.

It was no great loss, since she had retyped the old scribbled notes that had accumulated all week. But now she had no paper, and no one to borrow from. The only other person there was a fragile old gentleman, his back to her, his slightly humped shoulders bent over a magazine by the window.

I should go over and tell him he needs better light to read by. She smiled at the thought, remembering the many times she had heard that admonition as a child.

She walked up front to the card catalog and took a handful of the small pieces of paper left there for anyone's convenience. Though scrappy, they would do, since her shorthand system got a lot of words in a small space. She took notes quickly, wanting to get home in case Mrs. Sieverson was back and wanted something done.

She looked for the notebook on the way back through the library. It was not there or on the steps outside the wide front doors. Probably some kid had found it and now had a practically new notebook for school.

She started along the sidewalk, enjoying the crisp chill of the air and the sound of her feet scuffling through heaps of drifted leaves. The walk home was long, long enough to take a bus but not cold enough for that.

"Hi! Going my way?"

The words came with the quick, sharp sound of a car horn. Katie looked over at the red car. The top was up this time, and Barry had a cheerful grin. She walked over to the curb.

"Yes if you are headed home. That's where I'm going."

"You feel that comfortable there now? To call it home, I mean?" He grinned at the faint color of embarrassment in her cheeks, and added enthusiastically, "That's great. Aunt Sigrid has that way with people. Especially if she takes a motherly interest in them, as she seems to have with you. Come on, hop in and I'll run you out."

As she fastened herself into the seat belt, he looked at her with a quizzical expression. "I didn't expect to see you coming out of that building anymore. You aren't doing double duty, are you? Working for Mrs. Sieverson and at the library too?"

"No. I came down to check a couple of books. I needed some facts and quotes to make a paper authentic."

"They don't have books in the university library anymore?"

"I'm used to these," she answered his teasing

103

smile. Then she added, feeling oddly defensive, "I'm not really *working* for Mrs. Sieverson either. She doesn't give me all that much to do."

"You mean she is not having you write constantly, 'Dear Joe and Martha, I pray for you every day while you labor so faithfully to give the gospel to the poor heathen'?"

He quirked an eyebrow at her and she replied hotly, "Don't make fun of her!"

"I'm not! I'm not!" He flashed her an amused glance. "So she's got you converted already."

When she did not answer, he sobered. "I'm sorry. I shouldn't have joked about it. Her faith means everything to her. It's the one thing that has kept her serene through the years. And, of course, as a Sunday school kid from way back, I naturally agree."

Katie glanced at him. Was he serious? Did he too believe as devoutly in God as Mrs. Sieverson did?

He went on talking, and Katie listened, glad for the security of the seat belt as he swung through traffic, flashing the car past street signs and trees and lawns.

"You've probably discovered that she has had a lot of sorrow in life because of all she's gone through with Lars and other things."

"She has said a little. She talks occasionally about the past, very briefly, in snatches, and she has shown me some pictures. I have the feeling that the sad events of the past are still very alive in her mind. But maybe that's because you had already told me about Lars."

"Yeah, I've seen some of those old pictures. Horrible dresses and hats the women used to wear.

104

Though as I recall, Aunt Sieverson usually looked nice—motherly, if not stylish."

Then Barry's amused tone sobered. "But she's not told you anything about the accident? Shown you newspaper clippings? Let you see letters?"

Katie shook her head, said, "No," and let it stand, hoping he would not ask any more questions.

But he had already moved in thought to something else as he asked, "Have you walked along the beach down below the houses yet?"

"No! It looks too wild down there."

"It really isn't, not when you are down there. It just looks that way from high up. Let me show you," he said impulsively. "Let's go now while there is still plenty of light and you can see how beautiful it really is. A little wild maybe, but not scary. How about it?"

"Umm—well—I—I really should go back to the house to see if Mrs. Sieverson is home and has something she wants me to do."

Barry shrugged his acceptance. "Okay, if you insist on putting duty before pleasure, we'll run up there first."

He shot the car along the quiet street, turned into the driveway, and swept to a stop in front of the massive front doors. As Barry turned off the ignition, Laila came out the door with letters in her hand. He put his head out the open car window.

"Laila! Is Mrs. Sieverson home?"

"No, she went out for lunch and isn't back yet." She looked from him to Katie and back again. "Why?"

"I want to walk Katie down along the shore, and

105

she thinks she should be in the house with her nose to the grindstone."

Laila looked at Katie, her green eyes narrowing, and lifted her chin, a cynical smile curling her lips. "There's nothing *she's* doing that can't be delayed for half an hour—or a week."

She turned and walked down the driveway, the fall breeze lifting the shining, white-blond hair that spilled to her shoulders. Katie watched her out of sight around the curve of the driveway and half smiled at Barry. "I'm not her favorite person as you can see."

"Oh, Laila's got psychological problems" he answered with a shrug and reached to start the car.

"Wait a minute. I'd like to take these books in. Be right back."

She ran hurriedly into the house, up the stairs to her room, and back down. Barry whipped the car around and drove back down the driveway, passing Laila with a brief toot of the horn and a careless wave. He sped along the street and around its curve toward the shore.

Maybe I can find out more about Laila from him, Katie thought as she glanced at him, sitting relaxed behind the wheel. "I've taken enough psychology courses to know that everyone has problems."

He grinned. "Yeah, the 'everyone's crazy except me and thee, and sometimes I'm not so sure about thee' syndrome."

He sobered almost instantly. "No, but Laila's are real. You see, she's got a hangup about living in this house. Her grandparents were servants here when they first came over. They were young and newly

106

married. Only—well—" He stopped, frowning in thought. "*Servants* is too mild a word. They were really slaves, because the old man was quite a tyrant. I mean great-grandfather Sieverson. This was back somewhere before the turn of the century."

"What do you mean by 'slaves'? Surely they got paid. Couldn't they just quit?"

"Oh, no! No, no. Old Mr. Sieverson had paid their way over, and they owed him. They didn't know they had any rights, and they couldn't speak English, so they couldn't ask anyone for help—were afraid to. The grandfather—that is, the husband—died not too long after they came over. The grandmother and her son, Laila's father, slept on cots in a little partitioned-off place in the attic, cold in winter and blazing hot in summer. Nobody else knew how they were being treated—"

"How terrible!"

Barry waved a hand. "There's a lot more to the story than that. Old man Sieverson was a mean guy from all I've heard."

"But Mrs. Sieverson told me the family was liked and respected."

"Oh, well, of course he wasn't typical of all the family. He was a throwback to the first one who came over. Maybe she'll tell you about him sometime if she talks to you about the family."

He stopped as if he were waiting for an answer from her and then went on. "Most of them were philanthropists of one kind or another. He's proof that the family isn't perfect." He softened the satisfaction in his voice by adding, "But then, nobody is."

A thought at the edge of her mind said, *Some jealousy there.* But aloud she asked, "But then, where does all the church-going come in? The two things don't fit."

Barry chuckled. "This same old guy who had been so mean all his life went off to a lumber camp when he was about 70 or so just for the fun of it. While he was there he 'got religion' as the newspapers say, from some old camp preacher. So then he came back and made everyone else start going to church, whether they wanted to or not. He was still mean, but just in a different way."

He laughed but with a tightness in his voice that puzzled Katie. "Anyway, ten years or so ago Mrs. Sieverson somehow discovered Laila. When she found Laila was a granddaughter of people some Sieversons in the past had treated so unfairly, she brought her here to live and treats her like one of the family. Laila wasn't crazy about coming, but it's an easy life."

"So her psychological problem is that she can't forgive the injustice done to her grandparents. But surely she doesn't hold that against Mrs. Sieverson?"

"Well—who knows what makes people do what they do?"

Barry lifted his shoulders in a lazy shrug as he answered and then said, "But enough of that. I'm parking the car here, and we'll walk along the shore down to that big pile of rock jutting up at the edge of the lake. See it?"

Katie nodded and followed him out of the car, feeling the lake wind whip her hair back and sting her cheeks. It was an exhilarating feeling and made her glad she had come.

Barry led the way along the shore a few yards and then dropped back to walk beside her, his hand under her elbow as he pointed out places on the far side of the lake that she could barely see.

"When the fog rolls in, you wouldn't know anything was over there," he observed, and leaned to pick up a stone to skip.

The sun, bright for such a late fall day, reflected out on the lake as though the water were a polished mirror. But near the shore where the massive tower of earth and rock shut out the sun, the water looked angry. It washed up around the rocks at the shore's edge, curling around each one hungrily and then falling back to gather strength for another attack. Katie turned to look up at the cliff. The houses could not be seen, and they seemed lost from civilization. She felt the same forboding chill she had had when she first stood in the security of the warm, lighted room and looked down on the shore. The bare rock stood silent, waiting.

She glanced up at Barry's handsome profile, and he felt the look and smiled down at her. "You see? Absolutely nothing to be afraid of. There's nothing here but silent, inert rocks and grass, and poor, stunted trees that never get enough sunlight to grow properly. Poor things. You can't blame them for what is not their fault." His voice was light and teasing as he reached out and patted one of the black, slippery rocks.

Katie pulled her heavy sweater closer around her

and turned up the collar. "Well, but you are used to it."

His face sobered instantly, the smile wiped off as though it had never been there. "Yes, that's true. I grew up with the scene. All of us kids lived down here by the water. Played pirates, pretended we were shipwrecked sailors, learned how to swim—"

"In there?" Katie shivered as she looked at the dark, swirling water.

"No no! We didn't learn here. There are safer places farther along the shore, down closer to the place where our house is built. But when we were good enough swimmers, and if there were a couple of adults around for extra safety, we were allowed to go in here. It is just unsafe enough, because of an undertow a little farther out, to be exciting to kids. You know how kids are, they never think of danger. And of course there's the forbidden fruit idea, which some people never outgrow."

He fell silent, and turned his face away. He dug with his heel at the hard ground. His voice was tired and heavy when he spoke again. "Our parents were very stringent about rules, especially after one poor kid, a friend of Lars, almost drowned. The family used to come to visit every summer, but after that they never came again."

Katie could tell from the somberness of his voice that the memory was still vivid to him. She wanted to ask if this was where Lars had slipped out of sight, caught perhaps by the treacherous undertow, but she did not want to arouse even more painful memories.

So she touched his arm briefly and said, "Thanks for bringing me. I can see there really isn't anything to be afraid of down here. But it is so gloomy I still wouldn't choose it as a place to picnic."

She stepped carefully along the uneven ground on the way back to the car, avoiding the slippery rocks.

"I'm glad Aunt Sieverson found you," Barry said as he helped her into the car and stood looking down at her.

The tone of his voice made Katie look up at him quickly and then away, liking the sparks of admiration she saw in his eyes.

"I'm glad too," she answered lightly and watched his muscular figure go around the car and slide in beside her.

"I'll have to reverse and go back the way we came since no other street goes through. You can see how secure the two houses are. There's no outlet at the other end of the shore for miles beyond our house. And there is no access to the houses from the back since only a monkey could scale that cliff."

"That was the reason for the houses being built there, wasn't it? For protection?"

Barry looked at her. "Apparently Aunt Sieverson has told you some of the family history after all."

"A little. I suppose I will hear more as she gets to know me better." She started to add, "And when we start writing the history," and then did not. It was Mrs. Sieverson's secret project, not hers to speak of.

Barry's hands tightened on the wheel and he shook his head. "Katie, don't let her get started too much on what happened in the past, especially to

Lars." His voice was unsure, groping. "The time for her to have talked it all out was when it happened. I was too young to know much of what went on. But apparently she bottled it up inside, kept her grief to herself. Now she really ought not to think about it. She ought to let the past alone. She can't change what has happened so she ought to let it rest."

He turned his head and smiled at her and put out one hand to cover hers for a moment, tightening his fingers around hers.

"I made you mad that day when I implied you were a stray kitten. I really didn't mean it then and I don't now, because I can see you are good for Aunt Sieverson. She may be helping you financially, but you are helping her in other ways. She apparently is already thinking of you as a member of the family if she is trusting you with family secrets. Keep that in mind and help us protect her, will you?"

Katie nodded wordlessly, touched by the compassion in his voice.

They were silent during the rest of the ride home, back around the curve of the big sentinel rock and up the slight rise of the street. Barry pulled to a stop with that sudden rush, as though it were a last-minute decision.

"Thanks for settling my fears," Katie said lightly as she got out of the car and shut the door, leaning to speak through the open window. "Now maybe I can look down on that frightening drop from inside without feeling that spooks are out to get me."

He laughed back at her and lifted his hand in a wave before rushing the car along the driveway.

112

Katie ran up the wide steps and into the house, feeling its welcome as she always did when the heavy doors closed noiselessly behind her, shutting her into their security. She went softly up the carpeted stairs to the light and welcome of her room.

Opening the door, she stopped. An alien presence was there—had been there—leaving a trace of itself behind.

EIGHT

She stood in the doorway, trying to pin down what made her so sure someone had been in the room in the hour since she had run up and dropped her books on the desk. Nothing seemed to have been disturbed. The white crocheted bedspread was unruffled, the pile of blue pillows against the white headboard just as she had left them. The desk was clear; pencils and pens still stood neatly in the blue, hand-painted vase, and the rocking chair was in place. Then she knew. It was the lingering fragrance of perfume, the kind of perfume Laila always wore.

Katie narrowed her eyes in anger at the thought of Laila's coming into her room in her absence and snooping in her things. She crossed quickly to the small blue desk and pulled open the drawer where she kept her checkbook. It was there. So was the envelope Mrs. Sieverson had handed her late Saturday with an apology.

"Katie, unless you really want your salary in a check, may I give it to you in cash? I thought you might need money, and the banks are closed."

Her voice had sounded hesitant, even evasive Katie had thought, and she had been quick to reassure her. "That's very thoughtful of you. Yes, I do need to buy some things, and having cash on hand will save me time on Monday."

She had put the envelope in the drawer with just a quick look inside, not even taking the money out, expecting it to be safe. She snatched up the envelope and felt for the money, relieved to find it was still there. It would be awkward to accuse Laila of stealing. Closing the desk drawer, she frowned and looked around the room. Nothing seemed to have been touched. Why had Laila come in? She had to have been in the room; the traces of perfume were too strong to have just drifted in as she went by.

Finally she shrugged the incident away. Probably it was just curiosity to look through her clothes or check her cosmetics, and the heavy scent had lingered.

She threw wide a window to let cold air sweep the room. Standing for a moment to breathe the freshness, she glimpsed the red roof of the Jorgenson house, and it brought thoughts of Barry. She felt again the excitement of his apparent interest in her in the moments he had helped her into his car.

She stood by the window, thinking. Had his meeting her downtown been accidental, or had he seen her go in to the library and purposely waited for her, wanting a chance to develop a friendship? Laila had not been too happy when she saw them together later. If she and Barry had once dated, naturally she would be jealous—

116

Katie turned impatiently. How ridiculous to imagine a romance just because a man took her for a casual walk along the lake! She thought back over their conversation, remembering Barry's almost off-hand telling of Laila's story. His story of the Sieverson history was a contrasting picture to the one Mrs. Sieverson had given. What dark currents swirled within a family from one generation to the next! She shivered in the chill of the room as the wind came in. It was not warm now that the sun had set.

At dinner, she tried to smile at Laila with genuine interest, wanting to say, "I would like to help make up for your little grandmother's having been shut out of love and home. I know now why you have such resentment, and I would like to be friends."

But Laila simply stared back at her across the table, her heavy lids not covering the dislike in her green eyes. Her white skin looked transparent against her black sweater. A narrow black velvet ribbon held her hair back from her face.

She is striking. Any man would be attracted to her. I wonder how Andrew really feels about her.

Katie watched them as she listened to the table conversation, letting it flow around her without trying to take part.

Andrew was describing a man who had come into the bank to open an account and had insisted on knowing all about the bank's assets. Afraid of turning away a potentially important account, someone took the man in to see the president.

"Turned out he only wanted to deposit $59.62." Andrew chuckled.

"Why so little?" Laila asked.

"That's all he had."

"Oh."

Laila's flat, uncomprehending tone made Katie reach for a glass of water as she choked, trying to hide a smile. She felt Laila's angry look as Andrew added, "Of course, $59.62 of real money is better than a thousand fake bills."

Laila still looked puzzled, and Katie saw the quick look Mrs. Sieverson gave Andrew, warning him not to tease her. She smoothed the awkward moment by asking, "Katie, are you busy this evening?"

"I have a paper to finish. If I can collect my scribbled notes tonight, it will take only a few hours to type it up. Then I'll be free all tomorrow afternoon."

When she knocked on the study door after lunch the next afternoon, she said, "Mrs. Sieverson, I *must* talk to you about the amount you are paying me. It is too much when you are giving me my room and board too. I'm not doing enough for you in return."

"You should let me be the judge of that. You have been with us only a few weeks and you have needed time to feel at home. The room you are in is not being used anyway, and the little you eat does not show on the grocery bill. Or on you either," she added with a light laugh. "Remember, our writing project cannot begin until we feel comfortable with one another."

She looked at Katie and, as though she were thinking out loud, she said, "I must still prove to Andrew that I am right about you. That you can be trusted."

As Katie drew back, her face showing her hurt, Mrs. Sieverson moved quickly to put her hands on Katie's

118

shoulders. Her voice was colored with regret. "My dear, I am sorry. I should not have said that, certainly not without giving you an explanation for it. And I cannot do that just yet."

She looked at Katie, her eyes expressing her dismay, and went on, "You see, Andrew's business makes him suspicious of every—well, let's say every unexplained incident, things that happen for which there seems not to be a logical reason. As a result he is in danger of seeing everyone as a potential criminal poised on the brink of breaking trust with someone."

She walked over to look out the window into the garden where a few late fall flowers turned greedy faces to the sun. Her words came slowly. "And, of course, in God's sight we are sinners, all of us, and in need of forgiveness. That is why none of us can be judgmental of others. We must all learn to forgive, hard as it is sometimes."

Katie moved impulsively to stand beside her, wishing for words that would lift the bleakness of the thought. But as she looked out the window, she exclaimed, "Why, I never realized before that this room does not look out on the lake!"

She regretted the words at once as Mrs. Sieverson's quiet voice answered, "This room was added for me. There was a long time when I did not want to see the lake." She turned. "Shall we begin?"

They worked together the rest of the afternoon with Katie sorry for her thoughtless words.

The cold wind off the lake cut through her sweater and raincoat as she stepped out the front door the next morning. She could not put off any longer getting a warm coat. She stood on the front steps, trying to decide what to do. Finally she turned, went back inside, and ran quickly upstairs. She debated whether to write a check if she found a coat she liked, and finally decided to pay cash since the money was still in the envelope in the desk drawer.

Just after she turned off the second landing on her way downstairs again, she heard Mrs. Sieverson's bedroom door open and Andrew's voice finish a sentence.

". . . expected something to have turned up by now."

And Mrs. Sieverson answered, "I am as convinced as I have been all along that she has absolutely nothing to do with it."

Not wanting to be caught eavesdropping, Katie hurried down the stairs and let herself noiselessly out the door, but the words hounded her. They had been talking about her, she was sure of it. But why? About what? *I've got to talk to someone about it.*

Hurrying into the academic building, she caught sight of Jane coming out of the lab and waited for her.

"I'm going down to shop for a coat this afternoon. Have you time to walk with me?"

"Sorry. I've got lab all afternoon—a really tough experiment. Can you do it tomorrow?"

"No, I have to go today. Listen, eat lunch with me tomorrow, will you? I really need advice."

The problem followed her through classes and then downtown, keeping her from enjoying shopping. After trying on several coats, she decided on a

120

long, belted one with a hood she could pull up for extra warmth on the bitter days ahead.

"Cash," she answered the clerk's question and took five twenty dollar bills from her wallet. The clerk took them, returned the change, and started to box the coat.

"Wait—I'd better wear it. If you'll put my other coat and books in the box instead, they'll be easier to carry. I have quite a long walk."

Coming out of the store, she huddled into the coat's warmth, buttoning it securely around her throat, and tossing one end of the long plaid scarf over her shoulders. Scuffling along through the few remaining red-gold and yellow leaves that crunched under her feet, she felt like a child coming home from school without homework.

The street she followed bordered the cliff that towered so high back of the Sieverson and Jorgenson houses. Her steps slowed as she neared the house. She could not go in; she could not face the suspicion. She glanced at her watch. There was time to explore the neighborhood and get a look at Barry's house from the other side. She went around a long, curving block and came slowly back. There were no houses on the other side of the Jorgenson's. Instead, dark, forest-like vacant lots stretched for a block or more with bushes and twisted trees growing right to the edge of the sidewalk. Katie instinctively quickened her steps as she passed them, relieved to reach the openness of a tennis court that began the Jorgenson property and was bordered by an enormous, sloping lawn.

She looked up at the house. The windows on this side under the sloping red roof were shuttered as they were on the side toward the Sieversons. The house stood silent as it had from the first time she had seen it. She could not imagine Barry with his friendliness and quicksilver wit belonging to this place so shrouded and foreboding.

As she loitered along, she saw a car turn off a side street a half-block ahead of her and stop, the motor running. It was Mark's car. She quickened her steps, half-running, to catch up with him. She could see Jane's head as she leaned to peer past Mark, studying the Sieverson house. Then suddenly the car picked up speed and drove off.

Katie stopped, disappointed. They had not seen her or heard her call. *I wish they had. They could have come in and seen the place and maybe could tell me what's wrong with it.*

She hurried up the driveway, suddenly aware of how cold the air had become. The mailman was just plodding down the wide steps.

"You're late today?" She made it a question, knowing that Mrs. Sieverson usually had the mail sorted long before this.

"Yes, ma'am. Bureaucracy, you know. They've changed the routes. Took me off my reg'lar one, put the fellow who was here on mine. Then they'll switch us again soon's we learn these. All in the interests of efficiency and the public welfare, you know." He grinned at her from under his low-pulled cap, his scarf muffling his chin. "Hope I've left you some good mail."

122

He went on, and Katie watched him reach into his bag for the next batch of letters.

She stopped to take the mail out of the box, not looking through it since she did not expect any. Laila was in the hall as she went in and held out her hand.

"I'll take it."

Katie handed the stack of envelopes over and went upstairs to wash for dinner. She decided to give Jane a quick call and dialed on the upstairs telephone.

Mrs. Ireland's querulous voice snapped a tart, "She ain't here," and then, "Hold on. She's jest coming."

"Jane, why didn't you let me know you and Mark were driving out this afternoon?"

"You saw us? I-I mean, how do you know we were there—it was us?"

"Who could miss Mark's beat-up car?" Katie laughed and then listened to Jane's embarrassed explanation.

"Mark has this thing about gawking at rich people's houses. I guess he got it from his parents. They used to drive around in his dad's old pickup truck, especially at Christmas to see the lights and decorations in that part of town. So he just wanted to see—where—where you were—living—" Her voice trailed off.

"Jane, you and Mark can come over. Mrs. Sieverson has told me I could have friends in anytime. Tell Mark he can walk right in the front door and I'll give him a tour of the house from inside."

"We'll do that."

But there was something Jane was not saying.

Katie was sure of it as she put down the receiver and stood for a moment thinking of the conversation. Jane had been—well, evasive. It was not like her. She shook off the thought. Mrs. Ireland had probably been standing right there in the front hall, clocking her use of the phone, and she had not been able to talk freely.

Laila looked up at her as she came down the stairs. "You got some mail." She held up a plain, brown mailing envelope.

"I did? That's unusual." She opened the end of the envelope as she spoke and the missing notebook fell out.

"That's funny! Who would know where to send this—oh, of course. Miss Elder knows I live here. She must have found it." She looked at Laila in explanation. "I dropped this when I was in the library the other day. I don't really need it, but I am glad to have it back."

She looked beyond Laila then and saw Andrew standing in the study doorway, listening with such obvious attention that it upset her. She turned and hurried up to her room with the envelope and the notebook, biting her lip in perplexity. The notebook had not been on the table in the library by her bag nor outside on the steps. Therefore she *must* have dropped it by the checkout desk and Miss Elder had found it.

Not knowing I was there, she had simply decided to send it to me through the mail. She explained it to herself, but was not reassured since that did not explain Andrew's interest in it.

She stood by the little blue desk and looked carefully through each page. There was absolutely nothing there to interest anyone, nothing, in fact, anyone else could understand. All it contained were the notes on the Mexican War, and only she could figure them out. Maybe someone thought the notes were a coded message. Her eyes sparkled at the silly thought. It would be fun to slip in some innocuous message to cloud the problem and then casually drop the notebook again in the library.

She was still smiling when she ran downstairs for dinner. The ridiculous thought helped her to relax and look at both Laila and Andrew with amusement showing in her eyes.

The telephone rang just before dinner was over and Andrew answered, taking the call on the extension in the study. From where she sat at the table, Katie could see him standing at Mrs. Sieverson's big desk. His voice carried clearly. "Yes?—When?"

She saw him turn and knew he looked directly at her as he listened and then answered, "Just a minute."

He put the receiver down and walked over to close the study door. His voice became a distant murmur. To her left Katie could see Mrs. Sieverson crumbling a slice of cake on her dessert plate, her slender eyebrows drawn together as though she had a headache. Then Andrew came back.

"Sorry," he said, resting one hand lightly on his aunt's shoulder. "I have to run downtown on business. Something has—turned up."

The slight hesitation between the words was obvious. Katie saw the questioning look his aunt raised toward him.

He answered it by adding, "As we expected."

This time Katie was sure of the dismayed look on Mrs. Sieverson's face and felt the glance in her direction. She imagined even that Laila sat tense, her green eyes lifting for a quick look at Katie, before she excused herself to clear the table. Katie helped automatically, but neither of them spoke as they worked together in the kitchen. Then she went through the dining room to the study and looked in.

Mrs. Sieverson stood at the window, her back to the room. The darkness in the yard was intense, shut in by the trees at the far edge. Beyond, the Jorgenson house was an unexpected blaze of lights, except for the dark stretch at the top of the house which was the shuttered windows.

Barry must be having a party, Katie thought, and felt left out. She wished for lights and laughter in this house.

"Is there anything you want me to do this evening?"

Mrs. Sieverson did not turn, but spoke across the distance of the room, her voice tired and listless. "I think not. I want to do some reading this evening."

Katie walked slowly up stairs and into her room. She closed the door. The house was not a haven for her after all. Mists of suspicion were curling around her. Something mysterious was going on, something directed at her. She could not mistake the glances, the veiled words. The suspicions at first had been only annoying. Now they were taking shape and were beginning to frighten her.

She looked at the notebook on the desk. Its unexpected return must mean something. She picked up the envelope, hoping to recognize Miss Elder's old-fashioned, flowing script, but the address was typed. She went carefully through each page again. Only the first dozen or so pages were used, and they were filled with her closely scribbled notes.

Was there any connection here with those other notes she had pulled out of the book that first evening before she had met the Sieversons and Barry and everyone in this place? She had saved them intending to show them to Jane and Mark, but her unexpected move had made her forget them. Jane had suggested she mail them, but she had forgotten again. Could they possibly be important in this mystery? She hunted for them through the pocketed folder she had used for the notes for the research paper.

"I must have thrown them away after all," she muttered. She leaned back in the chair, drumming her fingers on the desk.

The waiting sense of anxiety made her restless, unable to concentrate. She read several chapters for history but finally quit, not sure what she had read. "I might as well get some sleep and read this in the morning." The sound of her own voice was reassuring as she moved around the room getting ready for bed.

She turned out the light and walked over to pull up the window shade to the view of the stars in the night's darkness. "I am the Lord that stretcheth forth the heavens." The words came unbidden from the afternoon's reading. She forced her mind away from them. Better to remember the verse from childhood—"Star light, star bright; first star I see tonight" and wish upon a star.

As she stood, reliving memories, a car motor started up somewhere along the quiet street and came slowly from the direction of the Jorgenson house, its lights dimmed. It stopped outside the Sieverson driveway and then moved out of sight.

"That was Mark's car!" She spoke out loud, a thread of fear lacing the words. Why would he be here now after dark, driving so slowly past the house? Jane's explanation could have fit the other time, but not now, not this.

Then words came back. Hers—"How about shopping with me?" and Jane's—"Sorry, I've got lab all afternoon." But she had not been in lab. Instead, she and Mark had sat in the car, studying the house. Why?

The night was quiet now, and she got into bed. Unreasoning fear made her pull the sheet up close under her chin. Lying stretched out, wide awake, her muscles tense, she stared out the window at the thick shimmer of stars beyond the tree branches. The vague unease she had had about this position right from the start had gradually been dispelled by the ease of the job, but it now crystallized into the certainty that there was something terribly wrong here. These people were not what they seemed to be. *And either are Jane and Mark*—and that was worse, for he had thought them friends.

She thought about each one. Laila. "I could believe anything about her," she said out loud into the dark. With her background and appearance and her sly way of watching everyone, she could easily be a spy. After all, did anyone really know what she did when he was gone all day and usually every evening? Mrs. Sieverson was so trusting. Did she or Andrew know who Laila's friends were? If she still carried a grudge for her grandparents' mistreatment, she could be doing something underhanded, aimed at the Sieverson family. *But that wouldn't explain the suspicions about me.* She turned restlessly at the thought.

What about Barry? She knew nothing about him except that his family belonged here and that he had grown up with Andrew and was handsome and friendly and fun to be with. And he liked Mrs. Sieverson, clearly liked her. He did not seem devious enough to be able to plot anything sinister. But of course he could have a dimension that did not show on the surface.

Andrew? Her mind circled his name warily. She admitted consciously for the first time how much she wanted him to think well of her. It seemed impossible that a respected, reputable businessman would be involved in anything crooked. Yet newspapers were full of stories about people like that being a front for a racket of some kind—even drugs. Anyone could be a pusher. It was always the person you least suspected.

But her mind thrust the idea away immediately when she thought of Mrs. Sieverson. No one could

129

lead a double life and be so intimately a part of he
life. She was too sensitive, too transparent, too muc
a believer in God.

Katie lay quiet, thinking about the unshakeabl
faith Mrs. Sieverson had in the goodness and love c
a sovereign God. It had kept her serene in the loss c
Lars and in other crises barely hinted at.

She remembered the day she had rushed ou
heated words, saying that what was going to b
would be. Mrs. Sieverson had shaken her heac
gently reproving.

"That's fatalism, Katie. That is not what believing i
God is. Believing God is knowing His way is best. It i
knowing that now and throughout eternity one i
safe in the Father's house."

The quick thought that had come then cam
again now. Was that true of her parents? Were the
safe like that? If it was true, as Mrs. Sieverson saic
that there was only one way to God, then they wer
not safe. They had never given God room in their life
had never admitted there was a personal God. Bu
how could such gentle, loving people be—lost?

She closed her eyes, forcing the question out c
her mind. That was too big a problem to handle nov
while she faced this other immediate one. She wa
surrounded by undercurrents of intrigue that wer
mysterious and threatening. And now Jane and Mar
were added to the puzzle. She would have to guarc
every word she said to Jane from now on and at th
same time be alert to her actions and words.

The silence of the house oppressed her as sh
tried to plan. She thought back to that original meet

in the library, trying to remember every word of the conversation, the glances they had exchanged. Whose idea had it been to invite her to live here? And why her? Mrs. Sieverson claimed she needed help with correspondence—but who had helped her before? Why couldn't Laila do it on Saturdays? The idea of writing a history had not been part of the original job offer she was sure.

And where did Jane fit the pattern? She had insisted Katie take the job. She had said, "Don't pass this up" and "Nothing could go wrong." Had she expected something to go wrong, *known* something would go wrong?

Katie shook her head. None of this made sense. Nothing explained why *she* was the one everyone was suspicious of.

"One thing I won't do is quit," she said grimly, her voice loud in the quiet of the room. "I'll stay until I'm forced out."

But the words spoken so emphatically brought no comfort and she slept restlessly, waking in the morning with a tired, heavy feeling. The day beyond the window matched her dull mood; the bright sparkle and color of the past weeks were gone as the weather got ready for the gloom of winter days.

When she went down for breakfast and looked out the kitchen window toward the lake, it was hard to tell where the gray sky ended and the dark, sullen-looking water began. Some gray days, even though gloomy, were gentle; this one was hard. Clouds moved across the sky menacingly, heavy and black.

The wind whipped branches and drove leaves across the yard.

Katie poured a cup of coffee and sank listlessly onto a chair by the kitchen table. This morning the coffee's fragrance had no appeal, and she had no appetite for the sweet rolls and fresh bread in the bread box.

She drank the coffee quickly and rinsed the cup under the hot water faucet. Going back through the dining room, she stopped for a moment outside the study door, listened, and then tapped lightly. There was no answer. After a moment she went upstairs for her coat and books. There was no sound anywhere in the house as she went down and let herself quietly out the front door. The bite in the air meant the walk to school would be cold, but she welcomed the chance to walk off her unease and doubts. Somehow she would have to avoid talking to Jane, get out of eating lunch with her as they had planned.

Dad always said I could never be a successful liar because my face gave me away. I'd better learn how now, she thought grimly.

The lethargy and dullness stayed with her and followed her into class, keeping her from the stimulation she usually got from the lectures and discussions. While aimlessly leafing through a psychology text, she found the cryptic notes she had shaken out of the library book by accident. She pulled them out and studied them. They still made no sense.

She did not dare give them to Jane after all. That might be playing right into her hands. Instead, on impulse, she wrote a couple of lines of her own

132

shorthand underneath whatever the original said. After her last class she went downtown to the library and back to the history section. It had been that dull Mexican War history that had started this whole bizarre thing. If she put these notes back in the book, perhaps it would end it.

Going through the library, she saw Miss Elder at the desk and stopped. If she asked the right questions, maybe she could find out more about the Sieversons and get a clue to her problem. But all Miss Elder did was gush over the family and exclaim how lucky she was to be living there.

"Right in the *middle* of *history*, my dear!" Her eyes behind her glasses were moist with emotion.

Finally Katie said, "Well, it was nice seeing you again. Oh, by the way, thanks for sending on my notebook. The one I dropped here the other day," she explained to Miss Elder's blank look.

"It was not I."

That unreasonable panic flared again. All the way home on the bus she asked herself who *had* sent it, and who knew it belonged to her. The answer was so obvious she could not help whispering it out loud— "Jane." But the question "Why?" had no answer.

She ran from the bus stop to the house and leaned against the door as she shut it behind her, breathing quickly from the run up the long driveway in the cold air. At the sound, Andrew came to the doorway of the living room.

"Come in a moment, will you please?"

Something in his voice froze Katie. She walked slowly toward him to look from his face to Mrs.

133

Sieverson and then to the third person in the room, a man in uniform.

"We'd like you to explain where you got this money." Andrew held several bills toward her, and Katie glanced at them. Three twenty dollar bills.

She gestured helplessly. "I—don't know. Why do you think they are mine? Why would I recognize them?"

"We got them from the clerk where you bough your coat yesterday."

"Why then—" Katie stopped and threw out her hands again. "They are—It has to be the money Mrs Sieverson gave me." She turned to her for confirmation. "It's the money in the envelope you gave me."

Before Mrs. Sieverson could speak, Andrew said sternly, "That is not possible. She gave you marked bills that were genuine twenties. These are counterfeit."

134

NINE

Katie stared back at the accusation so clear on his face, hearing the words but not understanding how they could be true.

"But—but—that's impossible!" she burst out. "I took those bills out of the envelope in the morning just before I left for school and then went down right afterword to shop." She turned to Mrs. Sieverson. "I took them from the envelope you gave me."

Then she remembered. "That is, I did before. I mean, I put some of my own money in the envelope and took some of the new bills out, because I'm always afraid new bills will stick together and I'll use more than one. I did that once. Lost money, I mean, because two tens were new—You know how money does when it's new? I put some of my money in the envelope because it was older—"

She stopped, panic building in her. Even to her ears the explanation was weak, and the repetition of the words was making her sound guilty. Then anger washed over her. "I can prove it, because I still have some of your money in my room. I'll get it."

She turned toward the stairs but the other man stopped her with a gesture. "That isn't necessary. Your still having the marked bills wouldn't prove anything. In fact, it might only prove that all you did was substitute the counterfeit money for the real and spent it."

"I tell you I used my own money! I don't know anything about counterfeit bills!" The words came in a blaze of anger.

"Then how did it happen that you were the one who gave the clerk these bills?" The police officer's voice was polite but relentless.

"How does she know I was the one? The stores were crowded yesterday. Lots of people were shopping. It could have been someone else."

"She remembers you. Remembers that you bought a coat and wore it home. She put your other coat and two books in a box for you to carry—as you asked her to. You gave her five twenty dollar bills. We were alerted several weeks ago to a counterfeit ring working this area. We've been expecting bills to turn up, twenty dollar bills. These are the first that have been reported."

Katie swallowed, staring back at him and feeling trapped. *I'll never again laugh at the idea of circumstantial evidence convicting an innocent person. This can't be happening to me.*

But it was. Everyone stood watching, waiting to pounce on her words. She could read the accusation in Andrew's eyes, in the officer's eyes. Even Mrs. Sieverson stood watching and waiting.

Then Mrs. Sieverson moved quickly and said, "An-

136

drew, I think we should sit down and talk this over calmly. We have not even given Katie a chance to clear herself. You have simply jumped to a conclusion. You owe her the courtesy of thinking she might be innocent. It is very possible that someone could have passed these bills to her without her knowing it."

She looked at Katie. "You said you had the money while you were at school. Could someone have had access to your purse?"

In her anger and fright, Katie was grateful for Mrs. Sieverson's trust. But she shook her head. "No, I had my bag with me every moment. No one could have gotten at my wallet."

The bulky officer standing by the window stirred and turned, answering Mrs. Sieverson. "That's not too likely anyway since these are the first that have actually been passed here. The only others that have shown up were in a town south of here. The report just came through."

He stopped and cleared his throat. In the momentary silence, while Katie watched and listened, she somehow knew instinctively that he would say, "The town was Rushford."

She felt Andrew's questioning look, saw the dismay in Mrs. Sieverson's eyes, looked from one to the other and repeated stubbornly, "I don't know anything about this. I only know I took money out of the envelope Mrs. Sieverson gave me and used some of my own money, good money. I have absolutely nothing to do with counterfeit money here or in—in—"

She stopped, afraid her voice would break if she said the name of the town.

"You did live in Rushford? You came here from there? You have a bank account there?"

"Yes, but I've been here since early in September. I haven't even been back there, so you can't connect me with that money."

The officer looked back at her stolidly. "The bills were mailed to the bank to be deposited in an account made out to—" He pulled a slip of paper from his pocket. "Miss Katherine Cameron, account number 630 092."

The words jolted her. That was her account number! But who would know it? To cover her fear, she lashed out, "Who would be so stupid as to send counterfeit money to his own account in a bank? For that matter, who would send cash through the mail?"

The policeman looked back at her, his jaws moving rhythmically around a wad of gum, his eyes steady on her face. "This person."

"I tell you I didn't do it!"

Andrew cleared his throat and moved forward, his voice showing his regret. "Katie, I should tell you that you have been under surveillance for some time—"

"Andrew! Don't!"

Katie looked from one to the other. Then the significance of his words and of Mrs. Sieverson's cry became clear. *That* was why they had her here. Somehow they had got the idea that she was a counterfeiter. The offer had not been, had never been from a desire to help her, but simply to watch her, to trap her. And she was trapped with no way to prove her innocence. It was her word against—what? She fought down panic and tried to think clearly. There had to be some way to make them see that she did not have any money, real or fake.

"You may search my room if you want to," she challenged.

"Thank you," Andrew answered gravely, and she watched him cross the room and start up the stairs. He stopped and looked at her across the long room. "You may come too. I would not want you to be afraid we might plant evidence."

She shook her head. "You won't find anything. There is nothing in my room to find. I know nothing about counterfeit money." Her voice was ragged in spite of her effort to hold it steady.

"I will come," Mrs. Sieverson said. She stopped to put an arm around Katie and look across at Andrew. "I do not believe you are involved in this. I am sure there is some logical explanation for it all."

But when they came downstairs a few minutes later, Mrs. Sieverson's face was troubled, her eyes dark with shadows of worry. She thrust out her hands in a gesture of appeal as she looked at Katie and said, "My dear, I am sorry."

Katie looked from her to Andrew, and then stared in disbelief at the thick roll of bills in his hands, folded over and held together by a rubber band. He held them out toward her, the question clear in his steady blue gaze. A stern question was there but also a warm shading of compassion.

Katie faced him, her chin up defiantly, her hands clenched into fists behind her back. She made herself hold her voice steady. "I don't know how I can convince you that this is all circumstantial evidence. I do not know how those bills got in my wallet, or in my bank account, or in my room. I don't even know where you found them. I know absolutely nothing about this."

"Sorry, Miss Cameron. I'm afraid you'll have to come along with me and answer some questions downtown." The policeman stepped toward her.

"Andrew!" Mrs. Sieverson moved swiftly to stand beside Katie. "You must not do anything rash. I agree with Katie that you have no proof she is involved. There is no reason she cannot stay here while you investigate further."

Andrew nodded at the other man, who lifted one shoulder in resigned protest and then reached to pick up his cap. They heard the door close behind him. Then Andrew looked across at Katie, and she returned the look. She still held her head defiantly. It was the only way she could keep from showing her anger and fear and keep the tears from spilling over.

The hint of concern and sympathy still showed as he said, "I'm sorry. But we do have to follow this through. You understand that we can't ignore any lead."

A lead is *not* evidence!" she retorted.

Andrew stood, tapping the thick pack of folded-over money on the palm of his hand.

"I want you to know that I really am sorry about all this. But you can see how the evidence fits together and seems conclusive—the money at the store, in your bank account, and now in your room. There is

140

no way you can explain it?" Hope was clear in his voice.

She shook her head, looking back at his troubled gaze. "If you would just try to find some other explanation for it instead of assuming my guilt!" she burst out.

"I'll do my best." He attempted a reassuring smile at her and turned toward the door. Then he stopped and looked back at her. "Would you be willing to stay here over the weekend? I mean, not leave the house? Can you miss classes for several days if necessary?"

"I'm under house arrest, you mean?" Her voice was bitter.

He looked back at her. His expression was so serious that she felt her fear deepen. "If you really are being falsely implicated, which is what is happening if this money is not yours," he gestured with the folded wad of money as he spoke, "then you would be wiser—and safer—to stay inside."

The seriousness of his voice caught her, and she nodded wordlessly.

When the door closed behind him, Mrs. Sieverson turned to Katie. Her soft voice was brisk and purposeful. "Now you and I are going to find the clues that will unravel this mystery. Let's go over every single fact we know. To begin with, I gave you five twenty dollar bills in an envelope last Saturday."

When Katie stood motionless, Mrs. Sieverson stopped and looked at her with a little smile glimmering at the edges of her eyes. "We have to do this, you see, because if you can prove those counterfeit bills are not yours, then I will have to prove to Andrew they are not mine."

Katie smiled back at her, blinking away the tears that now came with a rush in response to Mrs. Sieverson's trust. The tension she had felt under Andrew's intent questioning lifted a little.

"Let's begin again. I gave you genuine twenty dollar bills. And you?"

Katie took a deep breath, trying to relax, and repeated the story that now sounded thin even to her. "Because the bills were new and crisp, I knew how easily they could stick together. So I took out two of those bills and put two of mine, crumpled ones, in between the new ones."

"Did they seem different to you in any way? Feel different?"

"I didn't pay any attention. It didn't occur to me that anything would be wrong with them. I used one of them and bought—oh, odds and ends of things like a pair of mittens, a new lipstick, some aspirin."

"Do you know where you gave that money? Since it was marked, it could be traced."

She saw the expression on Katie's face, and shook her head in regret. "I am sorry, my dear. I did not like doing it, not trusting you. But Andrew insisted it was the only way either to prove or to disprove—"

"And now he is proven right—he thinks," Katie interrupted, her face showing her misery and indignation at the injustice.

"You and I are going to prove he is not right."

"Why should you believe me? You have no reason to."

142

"Because I have worked with you these weeks. Oh, I will admit that at first, before I knew you, I thought you could have become involved with counterfeiters without realizing the seriousness of it. But, in these weeks we have laughed together over the same things, felt sorrow over the same things, and—"

"People can fool you," Katie interrupted again. Her voice was harsh with the strain she was under.

"I know." She said the words quietly, and the expression on her face was still, guarded. She looked directly at Katie. "I have never had a daughter, but if I did, I would want her to be just like you—honest and sweet and lovely." She came across to Katie and put her hands lightly on her shoulders. "You lack only one thing. I have prayed every day since you came to us that you will some day have the beauty of holiness God gives to those who belong to Him."

The poignant words gripped Katie, and she could not keep the tears from spilling over. She wiped them off her cheeks with the back of her hands, not trusting herself to speak. She stood for a moment, comforted by Mrs. Sieverson's loving embrace.

Then Mrs. Sieverson turned and walked over to look out the study window. Her voice came slowly. "Tell me, when did you first meet Barry?"

Katie frowned, thinking back. "Well, let's see—"

"You didn't know him before you came to live here?"

"Oh, no. The first time I really remember him was the day you came in to interview me. He had probably been in the library before but I just had not noticed him. He's quite a science fiction fan, as I'm sure you

143

know, and when I checked out the books that day, I commented on them. He talked for several minutes. You know how much fun he is."

She watched Mrs. Sieverson as she stood at the window looking across at the red roof of the Jorgenson's house, seeming to be half-listening. She added impulsively, "Barry admires you so much. He told me he thinks of you almost as a mother."

Mrs. Sieverson made a short sound of protest and turned, her face twisted with grief.

Too late Katie realized the hurt of the words and said, "I'm sorry!"

"He probably has told you of Lars also then?"

Katie nodded.

Mrs. Sieverson sat down in the big gold chair. Her slender figure was almost hidden in it. After a moment she composed herself and smiled at Katie. "Let's go on now and think this problem through. Let's assume this all began with your meeting us and coming to live here."

Katie stood by the desk, trying to sort out the shadowy events that somehow would have to fit into a connected pattern if she were to prove her innocence.

She looked across the room. "How did you—" She stopped and began again. "What was it that made Andrew think I was involved in the counterfeit plot? I can see now that you hired me because of that, to keep a watch on me."

"Yes, it was Andrew's suggestion originally. All the banks in the area were getting reports of a large counterfeit ring working this part of the state. It was

144

supposedly operating in a cloak and dagger way with secret messages and—"

"Of course! The coded message I found in the library book! That must be part of it."

Mrs. Sieverson looked back at her, a puzzled frown creasing her forehead.

"You don't know about that?" Katie asked. "Andrew didn't see me take those papers out of the book when he was in the library and jump to the conclusion that I was mixed up in the scheme?"

"I don't think so. He didn't mention that to me." Mrs. Sieverson shook her head. "No, he got a tip, anonymously by phone, to keep an eye on the pretty librarian." Her eyes laughed at Katie as she added, "Naturally, knowing Miss Elder, we had to look for someone else. Andrew investigated the high school girls who help after school and on Saturday and they were cleared. That left you."

Katie stared back at her for a moment. Her attention was caught by something she had said. The words had a familiar ring, and she puzzled over them for a moment. Then she asked, "But who could have phoned him about me? Nobody here knows me. Even people at school don't really know me—except Jane and her fiancé."

There they were again. Suddenly everywhere she turned, they seemed to be a part of the problem. They could be counterfeiters. Jane was smart enough to work out a secret code. She had not seemed really interested in seeing the notes that day at lunch. She had rushed off, claiming to be in a hurry. And that would explain the returned

145

notebook—and the money in her bank account. Living in the same room had given Jane many opportunities to have seen her checkbook and find out her account number. The notebook had been returned by someone who knew her and where she lived. That fit both Jane and Mark. And they were definitely following her. She had seen the car twice. Both times could not have been accidental.

"Katie? Have you thought of a clue?"

"No—no. Go on—you were telling about the tip Andrew got."

"He knew I had been talking of wanting someone to help with correspondence. That part *is* true, you see. So Andrew suggested hiring you, thinking that having you right here would make it possible for him to watch you." Her voice was softly apologetic, but the hurt was so deep Katie could not help the flash of anger that came.

"He didn't mind bringing a suspected criminal into the house?"

She snapped the words, and Mrs. Sieverson protested, "Do not be too hard on him, Katie. Remember that he has a job to do. It would be terrible for the city's economy if it were flooded with false money. The small businessmen are in a precarious situation right now with inflation problems hitting them so severely. They could so easily lose everything they have worked so hard for. The officials in all the banks were terribly concerned to stop the counterfeiters before they could do much damage. Andrew felt—we both felt—that if you were not involved,

146

you would never know about our suspicions and we would have gained a delightful friend."

Katie wanted to blurt out, "But he showed his suspicions right from the start." Instead she said, "And if you found I was guilty?"

"Then I hoped we could show you that your life could be different." Mrs. Sieverson looked across at her. "Katie, I am going to dare to tell you something. Andrew has not spoken to me about this, not in words. But I have watched him grow up and I know him. He was so deeply disturbed when the telephone call came about you, that it puzzled me. I asked if he knew you. He said he did not but that he had chatted just for a moment with you in the library. I remember his words. He said, 'I cannot believe that anyone with such beautiful, honest eyes could be doing something so wrong.' It has been very difficult for him to be suspicious and on guard against you when he would so much like to be a—friend."

Katie looked back, finding no words to answer. Then she had not imagined Andrew's interest that first meeting! But a cautious voice whispered, *Wait. Don't rush this. Don't build hopes on such a fragile foundation.*

She moved to safer ground and said, "That explains why you kept insisting you needed help when Laila was already here. I couldn't understand that."

"She is not here as a worker. This is her home. I am sure you have sensed that her position here, her relationship to our family is unusual. Someday I will tell you more about it. She is a part of the Sieverson family history, as you will discover."

Mrs. Sieverson hesitated, and then, choosing her words carefully, said, "I do not want to interfere, Katie, but I do hope Laila is not influencing your taste in perfume."

"What do you mean?"

"I noticed when we went into your room a bit ago that there was the same heavy fragrance she always uses. It is quite distinctive with her, as I am sure you have noticed."

Katie turned, remembering the smell of the perfume. "That's strange." Her words came slowly as she groped to remember. "A couple of days ago—I'm not sure exactly when it was, I came home and noticed the smell of the perfume in my room. I noticed it especially because I had just come in from the fresh air and I could smell it very strongly—as though she had been in the room."

She stopped, looking across at Mrs. Sieverson, who had risen and stood gripping the back of the big, gold chair. "Was anything missing?"

Katie shook her head. "No. I was suspicious at first and looked at the money in the envelope. It was all there."

"*My* money? The same bills? Did you take them out and look at them?"

"Well—no. I just looked in the envelope. And I can't remember whether I had exchanged your money with mine before or after."

Then she caught her breath as the significance of the questions became clear. "Do you think Laila—Do you think *she* is a part of the counterfeit scheme? That she came in to switch the money? But she wouldn't have known about the envelope. Unless—unless she just meant to plant the fake bills. As she did today," she finished with growing excitement. "That *must* be how the money got in my room."

In answer Mrs. Sieverson came to her swiftly and hugged her, her voice high with excitement. "Katie! This may be just the clue we need." Then her mood changed abruptly as she stepped back, her face clouded. "Oh, but I do not want Laila to be hurt."

The words were a cry of dismay as she stepped back and looked at Katie, her eyes pleading for understanding. "Laila has had so much unhappiness and bitterness in her young life. You see, she has no refuge of any kind, emotional or spiritual."

She turned and walked back and forth across the room, her head bent in thought. Then she held out her hands impulsively in appeal. "Could you stand to be under suspicion a little while longer? Not say anything to Andrew about Laila until we have some really solid proof?"

"Does that mean you *really* believe me?"

"Of course. I never have doubted your innocence." Her voice was quiet but positive.

"But you have known Laila longer—better."

"Perhaps that is one reason I find it easy to doubt her. Laila has much in her past to make her what she is. I will not go into it all now. But I know what she is like—hard, self-centered, grasping. Yes, she has reason to be to some extent, I suppose, because of the circumstances in which she was raised. Psychologists would have a wonderful time analyzing her and laying all that is wrong in her to the tragedy of her heredity. And there is truth in that. But she has had other influences also, good influences, that she has deliberately chosen to ignore. She knows about the grace of God and His transforming power, and she wants no part of it. God, being who He is, never changes in His love for anyone, but neither does He force a person to believe against his will. The danger is that someday there comes a point of no return. constantly pray that Laila will not come to that day unprepared."

An intolerable burden of need overwhelmed Katie as she listened. In this respect she was no different from Laila. Someday she would have to face this question for herself. But not now. Not as long as a cloud of doubt shadowed her. Not until she had cleared herself of Andrew's suspicions.

Mrs. Sieverson went on, "You see, Katie, it is Laila's refusal to do right that makes it easy for her to do wrong. That is why I can see that she might allow herself to become involved in something criminal perhaps just for the excitement of it. The question is, who is in it with her? She is not intelligent enough to do the planning herself. She can take orders but not give them."

"We have first of all to prove that she is involved," Katie pointed out. "We can't just go to Andrew and the police and say we smelled her perfume in my room."

"Umm—yes, that is mere suspicion. And I have scruples against searching her room in her absence. It probably would be useless anyway, because she

urely would guard against leaving anything in-
:riminating there."

Mrs. Sieverson walked over to sit down at her desk.
She picked up a pen and looked at Katie. "Think of
every single person you have had any contact with
since you moved to town. Except clerks in stores, I
suppose. The one who turned in the counterfeit
money has been cleared beyond question. But let us
ist every name just to give us something to do."

"Well, I guess I'll have to start with Jane and Mark
since I met them first after coming here. I—I must
admit that the last day or two I have been a little—a
little suspicious of them. Although I don't know why,
eally," she added hastily. "I've thought of them
as—my friends."

"Have you any reason to change your mind?"

Katie looked down, away from the question in Mrs.
Sieverson's voice and eyes. They had lingered
around the house in a stealthy way, yes. But to accuse
them would be to do just what Andrew was doing to
her, using circumstantial evidence as proof of guilt.
She shook her head. "No, not really."

"We must check out everyone," Mrs. Sieverson
reminded her firmly.

"But not Jane and Mark. I don't even want them to
know I suspect them of doing something like this."

"But someone is."

The words jolted her with their truth. Not only was
someone a counterfeiter, but whoever that someone
was, he was deliberately, purposely, framing her. That
meant she must have an unknown enemy. But who
could it be?"

She thought about Mark and Jane again, and how little she knew about them. Jane had access to a lab and to chemicals, if that was what counterfeiters needed.

Mrs. Sieverson's, "Now who else?" brought her attention back.

"My landlady, Mrs. Ireland, who couldn't possibly be in a scheme like this. If she were, she wouldn't be running a down-at-the-heels rooming house. Then of course, other girls live in the house, but I don't even remember their last names now since I was there such a short time. Let's see—well, Miss Elder."

Mrs. Sieverson wrote down the name but laughed as she did and said, "I can imagine the look on dear Miss Elder's face if she knew her name was down on a list as a possible suspect in a crime. She would be crushed."

"If this were a story, she would turn out to be the mastermind behind the whole plot."

They both laughed, but Katie heard her laugh ring hollow as she realized that this was not a story but an actual event and that she was caught in the middle of it.

Mrs. Sieverson sat looking at her expectantly, her pen poised. Katie went on. "Well, there are you and Andrew." She watched Mrs. Sieverson write. "Then Barry, of course."

"How many times have you actually seen him?"

"To talk to?"

"Yes. Or—well, any time you have seen him, or thought you did and it turned out to be someone else?"

152

Katie thought back and answered slowly. "Once in the library, the time I told you he checked out the books, the same day you came in and talked to me. Then the next time was Sunday morning the day after I moved here. He drove by while you were in church. That's when I discovered who he is and that he lives next door. Then the next time, in fact the only other time, he brought me home from the library a couple of days ago, and took me for a walk along the lake behind the house—"

She stopped, seeing the sudden rigidity of Mrs. Sieverson's fingers on the pen and the alertness of her listening. Katie had noticed that mention of the lake always affected her this way, no matter what the connection was. But when she made no comment, Katie went on, "And that's all."

"And your paths have never crossed at any other time? You have never seen him when he did not speak to you, or you were not sufficiently aware to realize it was he? Perhaps even before you knew who he was?"

"N-no." Katie let the word slide out slowly while something stirred at the edge of her memory. Then she shook her head positively. "I'm sure those are the only times I've seen him." She looked at Mrs. Sieverson, her eyes wide and questioning. "You surely can't think Barry is behind all this? Why, you have known him all his life!"

"Remember, we are suspecting everyone. I have my name on the list too." She looked at the list again. "And these are the only people you have had contact with during these weeks?"

"Well, of course, I didn't mention my professors or other students in my classes, but I wouldn't know where to begin with them. A lot of them are simply faces to me."

"Umm—yes. I suppose it is possible that one or more of them could be influencing Laila. We do not know all her friends. We may have to suggest that Andrew investigate some of them, because we cannot rule anyone out completely. Is there anyone else whose name we should include for Andrew to check on?"

Katie gestured helplessly. "I've passed lots of people on the street while walking to and from school, people in the neighborhood, high school kids, children playing hopscotch. And, well—the mailman."

"I will add his name although there is very little need to. He has been on this route for so long he even recognizes the handwriting on the letters from relatives and remembers their names—"

She stopped as Katie stood up. "Not this one! This one was different, the other day, I mean. He was new. He said he'd been changed. The regular man was given a new route, he said." The words tumbled over each other as she poured them out.

Mrs. Sieverson's response was swift. "I am going to call Andrew."

She dialed his number quickly, and Katie listened to her breathless, "Miss Anderson, let me speak to Mr. Sieverson, please. It is urgent." She waited a moment. "Andrew, the mailman the other day on this route was new. Katie was just telling me—Because he told her—He said—" She looked questioningly at Katie and then repeated the words into the phone.

She listened a moment and then said, "Surely the post office would have a record of a switch in routes. Even if it is a routine matter, would not the employees have to punch a time clock or whatever it is they do?—Surely they would tell you if you told them it was important—When you find out, please call back, Andrew. Don't let us sit here in suspense. Thank you. We will be waiting."

She put down the receiver and looked at Katie. "He will find out for us."

"What would I do without your belief in me and your help?" Katie's voice was thick with gratitude.

"If it were not for us, you would not be in the middle of all this. I cannot help believing that you are involved in this because you are living here."

They turned startled eyes at each other as both had a simultaneous thought.

"The phone call about the librarian!" Mrs. Sieverson exclaimed. "That is what gave Andrew the idea of hiring you."

"Does he have any idea who called?"

"No. He did not recognize the voice. It sounded muffled, he said. I will ask him if he succeeded in having the call traced."

Katie walked restlessly around the room, picking up and putting down books and knickknacks, stopping to stare out at the Jorgenson's empty-looking house. Even though she was expecting it, she jumped when the telephone rang, and turned to watch Mrs. Sieverson answer. The change in her expression was clear, going from hope to disappointment.

"You are sure of that? No change at all on the routes?" Then she asked, "Andrew, did you ever discover who called you with the anonymous tip about Katie? You didn't? All right."

She turned from the telephone and, without looking up, said, "The post office said no one was changed on this route."

"Then why would he say that? He told me he had been switched." Her voice was stubborn and angry. "I didn't imagine it and I'm not making it up. I can remember his exact words. He said, 'They've changed the routes. Took me off my usual one, and put the fellow who was here on mine. Bureaucracy, you know. All in the interest of the public welfare and—'something else—oh, yes, 'efficiency.' I *couldn't* have imagined all that."

Mrs. Sieverson looked at her watch. "I know Mr. Johnson. He is home by now surely. I will simply call and ask him."

Katie hesitated, her voice coming unsure and afraid. "But—but—what if he *was* on this route after all?"

"Are you taking back what you just said? That he talked to you?"

"No."

"Then if Mr. Johnson contradicts you, we will simply have to look for another explanation. This may be more complicated than we expected, but we will not give up until you are cleared."

Hope and fear beat in Katie as she got the tele-

156

phone directory, and Mrs. Sieverson went down the list of names.

"It is a good thing I know his first name and middle initial or we would never find him in all these Johnsons. When I discovered long ago that he knew first names of all our family, I decided I would be equally friendly and know his and his family's names. Ah—here we are."

She read the number, and Katie jotted it down and then dialed.

Mrs. Sieverson took the phone and said, "Mr. Johnson? This is Mrs. Sieverson on Lakeshore— Fine, thank you. And you?—You have not been sick, have you? I have not seen you for several days and I thought perhaps you had been transferred to another route."

Katie stood, her hands gripped tight as she listened to Mrs. Sieverson's soft, friendly voice, hoping desperately that she would say next, "That's too bad. We will miss you as our mailman."

Instead, her voice flattened as she said, "Yes, I can see you have been on this one so long it would be hard to walk another route—Your feet would not walk straight. Yes, that is well put—Mr. Johnson—Mr. Johnson, you *were* here yesterday and left mail?"

She glanced up at Katie, who could hear his voice crackling an answer at the other end of the line. Then Mrs. Sieverson replied, "Yes, we do. She has been with us for several weeks—Well, perhaps this was her first piece of mail—Mr. Johnson, I am curious about something. Since we get so much mail here, how did

157

you happen to notice her name?—I see—Thank you. It was nice to talk to you—Goodbye."

Katie's shoulders slumped as she sat down in a chair and put her hands over her face. Her voice was dull and muffled as she said, "He not only was on this route, but he remembers bringing mail for me."

Mrs. Sieverson's voice was gentle as she explained. "He said he remembered, because with all the Scandinavians in these parts, it was good to have someone with a different name. He said—he said Katie Cameron was such a singing kind of name."

TEN

"I—don't know what—to say. I only know what he told me. I'm—I'm not making it up," Katie said finally in the silence that stretched between them. She looked across at Mrs. Sieverson and for the first time was really frightened at the spot she was in. So far she had been angry, angry and hurt at being unfairly suspected. Now, something that she had been so confident would prove her innocent, was doing just the opposite; it was drawing the net more securely around her.

"Katie, we must not give up. I believe there is some explanation for this that we just have not found. If you are so sure someone said those words to you and it was not Mr. Johnson, then logically it was someone else."

"You mean, someone *pretended* to be the mail-man?"

"Ah!"

Mrs. Sieverson's sudden, sharp intake of breath left her sitting rigid, her hands so tightly clasped on top of the desk that the knuckles showed white. Her

159

eyes, looking straight past Katie, were dark blue, shadowed by memory.

"Mrs. Sieverson? Are you all right? Mrs. Sieverson?"

Katie went around the desk and put her arm timidly around the still figure. At her touch, the stiff shoulders gradually relaxed, but Mrs. Sieverson's breath came in short gasps, and Katie could feel her trembling.

"Shall I get you something? Call someone?"

"No!" Mrs. Sieverson grasped her arm. "I am all right now. Sit down, Katie. I want us to go over this very carefully. Tell me everything you can remember about the mailman. What he did. What he said. How his voice sounded. Was he old or young?"

"Well, he was—" Katie floundered and stopped. "He was just a—a mailman. I've never seen Mr. Johnson, because I've never been here when the mail comes. This man was—well, I don't know! You know how it is," she pleaded. "You don't remember the person, only his official suit. His voice was blurred—as though he had a mouthful of something."

"Mr. Johnson does. Tobacco. He chews. Disgusting habit."

"He wore his uniform cap pulled sort of down low on his forehead. And he had a mustache, a big walrus type. Does Mr. Johnson too?" she asked anxiously.

"Yes, but remember, if this person was pretending to be Mr. Johnson instead of just any mailman, naturally he would try to look like him. And it is easier to put on a mustache than take one off. Mr. Johnson

160

always wears his cap pulled low—to keep the sun out of his eyes, he says—but he does that even when the sun is nowhere in sight."

Katie sat frowning. Her memory was nudging some earlier remark, but nothing came clearly into focus. Then she said, "Why didn't we think to ask him if he had actually talked to me? That would prove whether it was he I saw?"

Mrs. Sieverson shook her head. "No, that is no longer the point—whether it was Mr. Johnson or not. I am convinced that someone took his place. I mean by that that someone came after Mr. Johnson had been here, and pretended to be him deliberately, to do something. But what? Was this man tall? Fat?"

"I don't know!" Katie cried again, near tears. "I didn't really look at him. I was in a hurry, and we just brushed past each other. Even though we talked as I told you, I just didn't pay any attention to him."

"Did you actually see him put mail in the box?"

"No, I'm sure he didn't. In fact, he was coming back down the steps as I walked up the driveway. The mail *was* in the box though, because I took it out myself."

Katie sat down and propped her elbows on the desk, rubbing her forehead with her fingers. "I feel as though there is something, some clue just on the edge of my mind."

"The way he looked?"

"No."

"Something he said?"

She shook her head.

"Or did?"

161

"N-no. Wait! Yes, I remember. As he passed me, he said—said he hoped he had left some good mail for me."

Katie stopped, reaching to reconstruct the image that was just beyond memory. "Then, after he went by—no, *as* he went by, he reached into his bag, and I remember thinking how empty it looked, as though there wasn't anything left in it. It was just—flat!" She gestured for emphasis, her gaze coming back to Mrs. Sieverson's excited expression.

"And it should not have been! This is one of the first houses on his route, so he should have had a lot of mail left in the sack. Certainly magazines if not first class mail, since this is the time of month magazines are usually delivered. Now we can say for sure that someone took Mr. Johnson's place especially for your benefit."

"But why? Why for my benefit? Why not yours or—or Laila's?" Katie objected.

"Because we would recognize that it was not Mr. Johnson."

"But how could the pretender be sure you or Laila wouldn't see him?"

"He couldn't, of course. He had to take that chance," Mrs. Sieverson answered. "However, now we have something definite to tell Andrew."

"But he may not think it is proof of anything. I'm not sure myself what it proves. And anyway, it is still just my word against—"

Mrs. Sieverson interrupted with a positive shake of her head. "No, it is more than that. Do you remember what time you got home?"

"No. I wasn't paying any attention. I— was—thinking of something else." She stopped, remembering Mark in his car, Jane beside him, both staring intently at the house. Had they seen the mailman? Were they part of this plot?

She went on slowly. "It was not very long before dinner. I gave the mail to Laila who was standing at the foot of the stairs in the hall."

She stopped again—the scene was coming back to her. "I did have a vague feeling at the time that she was purposely standing there, as though she were waiting for something."

"You think she might have seen the mailman?" Before Katie could answer, she asked, "Or waited for *this* one, knowing who he was?"

Katie looked back at her soberly. "I don't know. I went up to wash, and when I came down, Laila gave me the notebook, and I went back upstairs with it. It couldn't have been more than a half hour before dinner. Why don't we ask around and see if anyone else saw this person? I could ask Barry."

Mrs. Sieverson gave a quick, protesting gesture. "Katie, I think we should go slowly on this until we talk to Andrew. Even a casual question to any of the neighbors could get them curious over something that is not their business. Do not say anything to Barry especially because it might get to his mother. Mrs. Jorgenson, as an invalid, is easily excited. It would distress her terribly if she thought there were danger in the neighborhood. She has been out of touch with the world for so long."

"I hadn't thought of that. And I certainly don't want the neighbors looking at me with suspicion."

Mrs. Sieverson stood, lost in thought. Finally she came back to the present, and worry clouded her voice as she said, "I do not want to frighten you, Katie, but do be careful. Please do not walk down along by the lake by yourself no matter how safe it looks. Too much has happened there in the past, unexplained happenings, some of them tragic. In fact, I would prefer that you not go there with anyone until this mystery is cleared up. Will you promise?"

"Yes, of course. But I am not physically afraid. If Laila is mixed up in this counterfeit ring and is trying to implicate me, of course I don't like it. But I am not afraid of her or her cohorts, whoever they are."

"Just promise you will be careful, as I will be. It would be wise not to trust anyone but each other. And Andrew." She patted Katie's arm affectionately as she passed her and went out of the room.

Katie watched her slim, erect figure go up the stairs and heard a·door close behind her.

I'm going to call Jane. The thought came with sudden decision, though she had no idea what she would say. Perhaps if she blurted out something about a suspicious-looking mailman and surprised Jane, her response might give some clue to the mystery.

She picked up the desk telephone, but before she could dial, she heard Mrs. Sieverson's voice.

"Andrew, Katie just said something that gives all that is happening a new meaning, a terrible meaning."

164

Her voice was so broken Katie scarcely recognized it. She put the telephone down quietly, not wanting to hear more, and stood by the desk, shaken by the anguish in the voice. What had she said to bring Mrs. Sieverson such distress?

She walked over to look out the window across the browning grass and turned it over and over in her mind. It indicated something more mysterious, more sinister, than just the business of the counterfeit money. She heard again Mrs. Sieverson's agitated exclamation at the mention of the phony mailman. She frowned, trying to think through every shade of meaning. It had not been just the idea of a substitute mailman that had bothered her. It was the pretense factor that had hit her so forcefully. Forcefully enough to call Andrew about it? Was that it? And, if so, why?

Her eyes, unfocused, staring through the window, were caught by a dark shadow at the edge of the grove of trees. As she looked, a figure moved, darting from behind one tree to the shelter of another. She drew back from the window, knowing the light behind her illuminated her clearly. It was still light enough for her to see someone out there; she could be seen much more plainly, however, in the lighted house. But who would be over there at the edge of the Jorgenson property, watching this house? Surely not Barry. He was a family friend.

Nervousness made her mouth dry, and she hurried to the kitchen for a glass of water, resisting the impulse to fling herself at the back door and lock it. Just as she took a drink of water, the front doorbell

165

chimed, startling her so that she almost dropped the glass. She put it down and walked slowly through the hall, looking up the stairs to see if Mrs. Sieverson had heard the chimes. The bell's melodious sound came again, and she rubbed her damp palms down her skirt before reaching to pull the door open slightly. Then she pulled it wide at the sight of Barry's cheerful grin.

"Hello! I'm just back from the shore, and I have to show you what I dug up. I remember you said once you always look for arrowheads. Well, look at this beauty." Barry held out his handkerchief, pulling it open to exhibit the arrowhead, wet sand still clinging to it.

Her relief at seeing his safe face was so intense she felt weak. Barry could not possibly have been down on the lakeshore and at the same time have been standing across in the trees watching her. She stepped out onto the wide steps to warn him.

"Barry, be careful when you go home. Someone is standing over there watching the house."

"Where?"

She led him out to the side of the house and pointed through the early dusk. "Right over there at the edge of the property. By those trees."

"Are you sure? I don't see anyone."

"Now don't tell me it's only my imagination," she snapped, her nerves so edgy that she felt irritable.

"Katie, wait a minute," he said, putting a reassuring arm around her shoulders. "I'm not doubting you saw someone, but you are probably making too much of it. It may have been just a neighbor kid

166

imagining he was an Indian scout. They do that all the time."

"Barry, what are *you* doing here?" The question from the open doorway was sharp, unlike Mrs. Sieverson's soft lilt, and they turned toward her in surprise.

"Aunt Sigrid, what's the matter? Don't you feel well?" The concern in Barry's voice was so clear that Mrs. Sieverson put her hands up to her eyes, shading them.

Then she looked at him and smiled a wan, tired smile. "I'm sorry. My nerves are a little jumpy."

"Is something wrong?" Barry looked from one to the other, and Katie had to fight back the impulse to pour out the whole story and ask for his help. But the plea, "Let's not trust anyone but each other," came back to her just as Mrs. Sieverson answered, "I have a little headache that makes me feel edgy and cross."

Barry shook his head, his smile rueful. "The only time I saw you cross, *really* cross, was the time Lars and I and a friend of Lars sprinkled sand all over the tops of the three hundred cinnamon rolls you had just baked for some church affair. We thought the sand sparkled just like the sugar you usually put on. We didn't stop to think that you would taste the difference."

He laughed, but his eyes were anxious as he watched her. She forced a smile, and Katie could see what an effort it was. She looked back at Barry, her soft voice reflective. "As I recall, it was your idea."

He nodded. "I'm afraid so. And I got a licking from my mother. And another one from my father."

167

After a moment Mrs. Sieverson said quietly, "You remember the sequel to that? Lars's friend got more than a spanking. He almost drowned."

Barry's face sobered. "I remember. And that was my fault too, at least partly. We were feeling so defiant at the adult world, all of us, that we dared him to swim out beyond those rocks when we knew we were not supposed to. Then we almost didn't get him out in time."

His voice trailed off into silence, and the three of them stood in the chilling darkness. Katie rubbed her arms and turned to Mrs. Sieverson.

"Brr. It's too cold for you to stand out here without a coat. You will get chilled." She looked at Barry. "Do be careful when you go home, because I'm sure someone was over there a little while ago. And I don't believe it was just a neighbor child. Your mother isn't home alone, is she?" Katie leaned to peer over at the dark house.

"No, my dad is home by now. But I'll scout around and see if I can find any evidence. I suppose detectives would look for footprints or crushed grass where someone might have stood. It's too dark to see anything tonight, but I'll look first thing in the morning." He chuckled. "Not that I would know how to interpret evidence if I did find any. Good night, ladies."

He turned away, whistling, and then stopped, looking back at them over his shoulder. "Wait a minute. You two aren't here alone, are you? I'll stay if you are and if you would like company. It wouldn't be the first

168

me I bunked overnight by my own invitation." He flashed his quick, bright grin at Mrs. Sieverson.

"Thank you, but we are not alone. Oh, Andrew is not here or Laila. But, Barry, you know God is." Mrs. Sieverson smiled back at him as she answered and then turned to walk up the wide, shallow front steps.

She closed and locked the front door and looked at Katie's troubled expression. "You don't think I should have told him we were all alone here?"

"Not because of him. We know Barry is safe enough. But someone else could have been out here listening, someone in the shadows whom we couldn't see. No matter what Barry says, I *know* someone was over in the grove of trees."

"Katie, even though someone might be out there and we are alone here, as far as human help is concerned, we need not worry. God is with us. I believe God when He says He will give His angels charge over His own, to keep them. I belong to Him."

She stood still as though listening, and then said, "There is a marvelous account in the Old Testament in the Bible about one of God's servants who was surrounded by a host of angels—shining angels, Katie—protecting him, angels his enemies could not see. You and I have that protection right now."

It should be a spooky scene standing here in the dim light with danger lurking just outside the door, and imagining unseen beings guarding us. But it isn't spooky. It's beautiful.

Mrs. Sieverson's voice became brisk and purposeful as she moved ahead of Katie along the hall, talking over her shoulder.

169

"Now we are going to be very sensible and lock a the doors and windows, and go out to the kitcher and fix ourselves supper from whatever the re frigerator holds. Andrew will not be home, so we ca please ourselves as to our menu."

"Will Laila come home tonight, do you think?"

Mrs. Sieverson shook her head, her face troubled "Probably not, if what we suspect of her is true."

They sat talking comfortably at the kitchen tabl over soup and salad and cold meat and apple pie. brought Katie memories of times she had sat like thi with her father. Their conversation had ranged over wide variety of subjects.

But God was a subject they had not talked abou except in a general way. Her father, such a lover c history, had been fond of quoting, "There is a tide i the affairs of men" with God no more personal t him than that. She remembered his quotin snatches of poems at appropriate times—after heavy rainstorm, he said gaily, "I saw God wash th world last night." When she railed at injustice h reminded, "Though the mills of God grind slowly, ye they grind exceeding small." And one of his favorit quotations was Voltaire's, "If there were no God, would be necessary to invent him." That was all Go had been to him, an invention. But God *lived* in thi house, and it was both a comforting and a frighten ing thought.

Later as they washed and wiped the few dishes she asked, "Do you really believe that God knows w are here, possibly in danger—and cares?"

"He would not be God if He didn't know, Katie. H

nows all things. That is wrapped up in the very idea f God. That is why He *is* God. And cares? Yes, of ourse."

"But we could still be harmed. Even people who elieve in God and His care get hurt."

Mrs. Sieverson's hands were still. "Yes, that happens often, Katie. We all wish God would show His ove to us by not letting any disaster or tragedy touch s. There is no easy explanation I can give you. I can nly say with the prophet of long ago, 'I know that ou art a gracious God, and merciful, slow to anger, nd of great kindness,' and rest in that knowledge. ften we learn this only by experiencing hurt and orrow. If we let them, the apparent tragedies are for ur good, to make us stronger."

She stopped, and then after a moment she said ainfully, "And sometimes disaster comes because e insist on going our own headstrong, willful way in efiance of God. He has a reason for His 'Thou shalt ots' just as human parents do."

Katie thought about Lars, skating where he had een warned not to. He had disobeyed, yes. But even o, God could have stepped in to spare Mrs. Sieverson such sorrow. Since He had not, did that not prove nat even if He did exist, He did not care?

She felt Mrs. Sieverson's steady look at her before he reached for a towel to dry her hands. "Katie, I peak from experience. Come with me."

She led the way upstairs, past Laila's closed room, a door at the end of the wide hall. She opened it nd touched a switch. Light flooded the room.

"My son's room," she said quietly. "Lars was just boy when he drowned—accidentally."

Knowing the story, Katie heard the slight hesitatio before the final word. She looked around the small clean, empty room. Shelves were crammed wit books, model airplanes, a large picture of a boy wit his parents, his arm around a collie. But it was not morbid room. In the daytime sunlight would pour ir sparkling the white walls and dancing off the ships o the wallpaper with its shimmering green water.

"He is gone, Katie. I do not know why. Perhap some greater tragedy awaited him if he had lived, and God spared him—and me—from that. He was happy boy and he belonged to God. I would hav liked to keep him, see him grow up, enjoy him now have grandchildren from him. But I would not inter fere with God's plan even if I could. I dare not doub His wisdom."

She looked around the room and said in her sof voice, "When God took Lars, He gave me Andrew Not in his place, no," she added quickly. "Andrew fill his own place."

The words rang in Katie's ears as she got ready fo bed. Then, lying still, her ears alert to every sound i the house, her muscles tensing whenever a branch scraped harshly outside the window glass, she made herself put these disturbing questions about God ou of her mind, as she had done before, by going back piece by piece over the puzzle.

Who had phoned to alert Andrew that she was par of the counterfeit ring and why? Where did Laila actually fit into the picture? What did Jane's and

172

Mark's mysterious stealth mean? And what about the mailman? Whoever he was, he had to be part of the conspiracy. Maybe Mr. Johnson himself was in it. Just because he knew the grandchildren's names did not mean he could not be tempted by an offer of money. For that matter, could Barry be trusted?

She tossed restlessly, finding the blankets too heavy. But when she pushed them back, she was too cold. Finally, her skin prickly with tiredness, she fell into a shallow sleep.

Loud noises awakened her, and she rose up on one elbow and listened. Someone shouted, "He ran out this way, I think," and a door banged loudly. Katie threw back the covers and reached for her robe, groping with her feet for her slippers, not bothering to turn on a light. She opened her bedroom door and stepped out into the hall to peer over the stair rail. Mrs. Sieverson was standing on the second landing, looking down over the bannister to the hall below, her robe gathered around her.

Katie ran partway down the carpeted steps. "What happened?"

Mrs. Sieverson looked up at her. "Someone broke into the house. Andrew did not see him until—"

"Andrew!" Katie stared at her. "Why, I thought he was out of town seeing about the counterfeit money."

"Apparently that is what he wanted everyone to think. He did not want either of us to know he was actually outside guarding the house. I did not know that when I told Barry we were alone. Andrew and several policemen have been outside since early

173

evening. They must have seen someone, but not in time."

A door slammed shut at the back of the house and they heard the sound of footsteps coming rapidly along the hall.

"That's Andrew's walk."

Katie followed Mrs. Sieverson down and into the living room and stood in the shadows of the room listening to Andrew's terse report.

"He must have come in in complete darkness without a light of any kind. That means he either knew his way around or had been thoroughly briefed so he would not bump into things and make a noise. We missed him completely. Did not see or hear him enter. Then we saw just a quick flash of light for a moment."

"But what was he—or they—looking for?" one of the policemen asked. He looked around with a gesture. "Nothing has been touched here."

"We don't know," Andrew answered. "We really didn't expect anyone to break in, at least I didn't. Maybe because we thought it was an unnecessary precaution, we didn't watch closely enough."

"Could it have been Laila?"

Andrew looked at his aunt as she asked the question, and shook his head. Compassion colored his voice as he answered. "Poor Laila. We know she is in on the counterfeit scheme; we have proof of that. But we have the place covered where she is staying, and she has not tried to leave. I don't know whether she knows we suspect her. If not, she may come back, especially if she has more false money hidden here.

After all, since she lives here, she could expect to come and go freely."

Katie listened, standing in the shadows, sure now that she was completely cleared in Andrew's thinking. Perhaps there would be time later to examine her feelings about him. Right now there was still a mystery to clear up, and she had to concentrate on all that was happening.

"She's got an accomplice, no doubt of that," one of the policemen said.

The other man broke in, "Now wait a minute. This looks to me like just a common burglar who has been casing the house and just happened to make a hit tonight." He took off his cap and scratched his head. "You'd better check your silver and other valuables, ma'am."

"The man watching the house!" Katie exclaimed.

"What man?" Andrew's voice was sharp.

Before Katie could answer, Mrs. Sieverson turned without a word and walked into the hall and through the dining room, snapping lights on the way, and opened the door into the little study.

They followed her and stood in the doorway, looking in shocked silence at the destruction. Desk drawers had been pulled out and the contents dumped on the carpet. The lock on the small wooden chest in the corner by the window had been forced open and the door wrenched so that it hung by one hinge. Mrs. Sieverson's big gold brocade chair had been slashed repeatedly and the padding strewn on the floor. Even the small, padded footstool had deep, savage cuts in the beautifully worked, cross-stitched top.

The police officer gave a low whistle. "Someone was either desperate to find something, or else simply wanted to do all the damage he could."

He crossed the room and squatted in front of the small chest, reaching in to run his hands across the two shelves. He looked back at Mrs. Sieverson over his shoulder.

"It's completely empty. Did he get whatever was in it?"

She shook her head, her voice coming unsteady, desolate. "No, I never kept anything of value in it. Only some old letters and personal mementoes which are no longer there."

"Nobody would want those," he grunted. "Proves it was a random burglary. Someone wasn't looking for anything special and thought the lock meant valuables were here. Then when he found nothing, it made him mad and this is the result." He stood up, dusting his hands together, and looked around at the destruction.

Shifting her position to see Mrs. Sieverson, Katie caught the expression on Andrew's face. He stared at his aunt and she at him. They faced each other wordlessly while some secret communication passed between them. Whatever the message was, it crumpled Mrs. Sieverson's face into silent tears while Andrew's kept a strange, tight look.

Mrs. Sieverson's overheard words on the phone came back—"It gives all that has happened a terrible meaning." What could it be?

ELEVEN

Katie looked around; a sick feeling grew inside her. The situation was getting darker and darker with no reason for all that was happening, no rational reason. She could see no discernible pattern to all this—coded messages stuck in a library book, counterfeit money, and now senseless destruction of private property. Laila could be a part of the counterfeit ring, but surely she would not have done this. Then who had? And, more important, why? Why ransack and destroy in just this one room?

She asked the question out loud and the policeman answered.

"Apparently our rushing in when we saw that quick flash of light scared off whoever it was. He may not have had a chance to get to any other room. Did you get a look at him, sir?"

"I didn't see a thing." Andrew's voice was harsh. "We should have waited a few minutes longer, not been in such a rush to come in. But I was afraid he would go upstairs—"

He stopped abruptly, the rest of the sentence unspoken but clear to everyone as they stared around at the viciousness of the destruction. If he was so violent here, what might he have done had he encountered two unarmed women?

Andrew walked over and examined the window. "He didn't get in here; the window is still locked. Either he is good at picking locks, or he had a key."

"From Laila?"

"Possibly." Andrew answered his aunt's question as he frowned over the problem, chewing at his lower lip. "While we rushed around here to where we saw the gleam of light, he must have gone out the back way."

The policeman shook his head. "There's no human way he could have gotten by us that way. Not unless he went over the cliff out back, in which case he's lying at the bottom down there, done in."

The note of grim hope in the man's voice made Katie shudder at what the sight would be of someone lying, crushed, on the rocks below.

Andrew paced restlessly back and forth. "That has always been the mystery," he muttered as if to himself. "That inaccessible cliff. There has to be some way—"

He broke off and turned to his aunt in appeal. "Will you talk to Laila tomorrow, if she is willing to listen? I'd like to handle this as kindly as possible. I still think that somehow, for some reason, she was forced into this business by someone and, if handled right, will tell us what she knows. If I or the police question her, she might only become more defiant and bitter. If you talk to her, she may respond to your gentleness.

She knows you have always wanted only what was good for her."

"Do you really think she will tell who she is in with?" Katie's voice showed her doubt.

"It's not just a name—she must give us proof," Andrew answered. He looked at his aunt. A worried frown darkened his face with apprehension. "You must be very careful what you say about—"

Katie saw Mrs. Sieverson nod understandingly at his broken sentence.

The policemen walked toward the door. "If you don't need us any more, we'll go along," one of them said. "Sorry about all this, Mrs. Sieverson. Miss." He touched his cap and went out.

Andrew stood looking around the room, his face both grim and sad. "I am sorry about this too. We should have been more alert. I didn't think about anyone getting in so easily. I thought we would see or hear something first."

"You think Laila gave him—someone—a key and described the room so he would know where to go?" Katie shook her head as she surveyed the shattered room. "How could anyone be so destructive?"

Mrs. Sieverson sighed, her voice full of regret. "It is futile to try to get answers to our questions tonight. We had better close up here and go back to bed. We can try to straighten up tomorrow." She walked over to pull together the worst of the deep slashes in the upholstery. "This chair needed recovering anyway."

"But the beautiful footstool," Katie mourned. "What a shame to have gashed it like that. He must have thought money would be hidden in it."

She saw again the quick glance that passed between them. But Andrew said only, "A person who would do this is apt to do almost anything to vent his anger and frustration. I suppose it is a good thing we broke in prematurely. He might have found his way upstairs to you two when he didn't find what he was looking for down here."

Mrs. Sieverson turned toward the stairs but stopped to smile over her shoulder at Katie. "We knew we were surrounded by protection that was far beyond what you could give us, Andrew."

"I believe that," he answered gravely. He looked at Katie. "May I talk to you for a minute?"

"Yes, of course."

She watched him cross the room to the foot of the stairs and look up at his aunt as she started up to bed.

"When I have checked everything down here, I'll come up for a brief talk if you are not too tired."

Mrs. Sieverson nodded, gave Katie a goodnight smile across the room, and went upstairs. Andrew came back, leaning to pick up some of the scattered papers.

"Will you sit down?" he invited politely.

She sat on the edge of a chair across from him, her feet primly together, her hands folded in her lap, feeling like a young, probationary teacher called into the principal's office.

Andrew stood leaning on the back of the chair with its ugly slashes, his long, strong fingers pushing at the padding, his eyes and voice very sober.

"I must tell you how sorry I am for the suspicions and false accusations you have been forced to live with these past weeks. I am especially sorry for my part in them."

He stopped but did not wait for an answer as he went on, "So many circumstances seemed to indicate your being guilty that I could not ignore them. I think my aunt has already told you that we hoped the suspicions would not show—"

"You are not a very good liar," Katie answered, remnants of indignation making her voice spark. "Your suspicions and dislike were very clear from the beginning."

He gave a quick, protesting gesture. "No, no! Not dislike."

Katie looked at him, startled by the vehemence of the exclamation. His eyes were clear blue now, the cold, guarded look was gone. "After that first brief chat we had in the library, I was disappointed when the accusing phone call came, pointing the finger of suspicion at you. I felt it had to be investigated since we had no other lead and the counterfeit money situation was becoming more and more serious."

He gave his slow smile, reaching out to her with it. "As usual my aunt was more perceptive than I. She agreed readily to your coming here, realizing that it would keep us aware of your actions, but actually being sure that your living here would show me I was wrong about you. She never doubted you for a moment." He looked across at her as he added, "She is very fond of you."

Katie nodded, her throat tight with the feeling that came whenever she was deeply moved. "I know."

"There is something else I must say."

Katie lifted her head, startled by the unsteady, groping sound of his voice. She had thought him so self-assured, so completely confident of his ability to cope with any situation, that she was not prepared for the uncertainty so clear in his manner.

"Living here these weeks you could not help seeing my aunt's deep faith in God. She is a Christian and lives her faith always, in every circumstance. It is so much a part of her that nothing can shake her complete confidence in God. My regret is that you have only sensed my doubts and distrust of you and have not seen in me Christian love and concern for you, and for that I am sorry. If my actions have made you doubt God's love and care for you, I do ask your forgiveness."

She could not question the sincerity of his appeal, and it touched her, though she did not want to explore this subject any deeper, not now. So she simply nodded and said, "I can see how you could have been mistaken. It is easy to judge someone on what seems on the surface to be true."

She was sure he sensed her withdrawal from the subject as he started to speak and then checked the words. After a moment he said, "Perhaps when all this is over, we could begin again without the suspicions on either side."

The unexpected note of laughter in his voice eased the awkward moment, and she stood, smiling. "I'd like that."

Katie said goodnight and went up to her room. She closed the door and leaned back against it. At last she was completely relieved from the burden of Andrew's doubt.

She crossed to look out the window. No stars were visible, and the moon was hidden behind clouds. Tomorrow was forecast to be a rainy day. *That means no footprints.* She smiled at herself for thinking like a policeman of footprints and clues. She got into bed and pulled the blankets up, lying relaxed and at peace. Finally she dozed off into a light sleep.

It was still dark when she opened her eyes, wondering what had disturbed her a second time. Then she heard the sound again, the mournful wail of the foghorn cutting across the night. She had not heard it ever except in her imagination when listening to the sea stories her father had loved. Now hearing it sent shivers over her just as reading about the sound so long ago had done.

She raised her head to see the time on the lighted dial of the clock. Two o'clock. Only a little more than an hour since she had come to bed the second time. She lay still, wondering if Mrs. Sieverson and Andrew were still talking, sorting out clues, trying to find answers to the questions they must be asking each other. She remembered the looks they had exchanged at unexpected moments. There was another dimension to this mystery, something they both knew or suspected. It was something out of the past. It had to be out of the past. Somehow Laila was part of it. Did she have brothers who were also angry at anyone who was a Sieverson and had come tonight to destroy?

She stared into the darkness, reviewing the bits

and pieces of the puzzle that to her were so disconnected. Yet all of them in some way must go back to those early days when the rooms and lawn had rung with the sounds of children at play. Then, Barry, Lars, Andrew, and other cousins and friends had explored the shore summer and winter until the awful day when Lars had slipped under the ice and left that empty room in his mother's heart and home.

A door shut quietly on the floor below. After a moment, another one closed. The house was still. But Katie was sure that in those other rooms, Mrs. Sieverson and Andrew lay awake, still asking questions. Had Andrew told his aunt that his questions and doubts about her were resolved?

"She will be glad," Katie whispered into the darkness that was warm and friendly.

She woke the next morning to a gray day. The sky was shrouded with heavy clouds. A chill blanket of fog had drifted in from the lake, muffling sounds. Only the doleful wail of the foghorn cut through the gloom to warn boats from the treacherous rocks.

It was Saturday. Even though she had not slept much, she could not stay in bed. When she went downstairs and out to the kitchen, it was impossible to see the other side of the lake. They could have been the only ones alive on an island of rain-bent trees, guarded by waves lapping on jagged rocks below. She smiled at her imagination. They were not, of course, because the Jorgenson house was a neighbor even though unseen, and there were other houses beyond other trees.

Someone had been up and eaten breakfast. She

poured herself coffee, and then looked around as the back door was opened and Andrew and Mrs. Sieverson came in, their raincoats wetly glistening. Mrs. Sieverson shivered in the cold that swept in with them through the open door.

"Summer is definitely over, Katie. Winter is on the way, though we may have a few days of reprieve with Indian summer." She gave her coat to Andrew. "If there is enough coffee, I would like another cup. Andrew?"

"Yes, thanks."

Katie poured him a cupful, lifting her eyes for a quick, timid glance. Did he, in the cold light of morning, still want to be a friend? His look back said, "Yes, I meant it. We are friends," and she felt foolishly happy.

He sat down at the table across from her, drinking the hot coffee slowly. "While just the three of us are here, and before we hear Laila's story—if she tells it—perhaps you would answer some questions, Katie."

She nodded wordlessly, fearful of what he might ask, not sure even yet that his doubts of her were gone.

He reached into an inner coat pocket and pulled out several sheets of note paper. "What do these scribblings mean?"

She took the first paper he handed her. "I haven't any idea. I've never seen it before."

"And this?" He held out a page and she nodded. "Yes, that's mine."

"What does it say?"

She shrugged. "This line is a quote from—let's

185

see." She took it from him. "Page 329 in my history text. It tells about a treaty ending the Mexican War. This line at the bottom is a quote from one of your friend's letters." She looked at Mrs. Sieverson in explanation. "From the ones who work in Mexico. It exactly fit a paper I was doing so I copied it. Their description of life among the ordinary people was so vivid it added authenticity to my paper. Did I leave this in the study?"

Andrew nodded and then said, "What about this?"

Katie looked at the paper he laid before her. It was the one with the coded message on which she had scribbled her own "answer" and put back in the book. She stared at it in surprise.

"Where did you get this?"

"From a book in the library. The police went through some of the books on Mexico because they had reason to believe there is some Mexican connection with the counterfeiters. They found this."

"And with my scribbles on it, it sealed my guilt?"

"Well, you see, I recognized your shorthand symbols."

Andrew's embarrassment and regret brought a smile, and she softened her voice. "That paper was in a book I was using in the library—it seems weeks ago now."

She stopped, hearing again Andrew's voice saying, "You need a Wednesday's child," and Mrs. Sieverson's, "Is there anyone like that?" Those words had begun the whole chain of events that

186

brought her to this place, sitting at the kitchen table so aware of Andrew's nearness.

She rushed the rest of the explanation. "I took the papers by mistake that day in the library, thinking they were mine. Before I put them back, I just added a few nonsensical lines in my own shorthand." She looked across the table at him, wondering if he would believe she had done it just for fun.

He looked back at her very seriously and said, "Unfortunately, we found it and thought it implicated you. Another piece of purely circumstantial evidence, of course, but you can see how convincing it made the case against you."

"I—guess I can't blame you for thinking me guilty," she admitted in a small voice.

"Tell me how you thought up the code."

"When I was very little, my father read me a story about mysterious messages. We worked out a ridiculous, just-for-fun code system. When I got to high school and then college and had to take so many notes, we improved on it for speed, and I have used it ever since."

"How does it work?" he asked. "What does this mark represent? And this? And this?"

When she answered unhesitatingly, he leaned back in his chair and looked at her. "So it really was all accidental that you found these notes in that particular book, had your own system of coded notes, happened to be seen by both me and the counterfeiters, and got mixed up in this—falsely accused."

"I do not believe it was accidental, Andrew," his

187

aunt interrupted. "But I am sure you built a case against Katie on circumstantial evidence alone. And it proves I was right about her all along." She smiled sweetly at him.

He nodded back. "I have already made my peace with Katie." He looked at her, his intense blue eyes reflecting his smile.

"I don't understand," Katie said. "Did you say the counterfeiters were putting coded notes in the history book? The Mexican War history books?"

"Apparently so. Why those particular ones we don't know yet, though the police are checking to see if there is some connection actually with Mexico. They don't have a report back yet."

"Well, I don't know when any counterfeiter could have seen me. There never are very many people back in that section."

"Would you know a counterfeiter if you saw one?" He looked at her, his teasing smile crinkling the edges of his eyes. Then he sobered and a frown creased his forehead. "A more serious question is why, knowing you were not involved, would they—or he or she—mix you up in it?"

"I have another question," Katie said. "When did you see my shorthand notes?"

"At the library the first time we met. You had a paper or a card of some kind with similar markings to these on them. Or at least I thought they looked similar. And, while we were talking, you reached out—surreptitiously, I thought—to cover them."

"They were only notes on titles and descriptions of books," she explained. "The marks looked so silly, and when I saw you looking at them—" Her voice trailed off as she looked down at the paper she had been creasing. Then she added, "I suppose then when you got the phone tip to watch the librarian, you remembered them."

"The tip was to watch the *pretty* librarian," he corrected her, laughing at her embarrassment.

Katie's mind groped back. Someone else had used those words before. It must have been he and that was why they sounded so familiar.

He sobered when Katie asked, "But who could have called you? I hadn't met Laila or anyone from here yet."

She broke the sentence abruptly, stopping herself from including Jane and Mark. She would not connect their names with this unless definite evidence showed up. It was too easy to accuse on mere suspicion. *I won't do that to them.*

Andrew was shaking his head as he folded the papers with the coded messages and put them in his pocket. "We don't have many answers yet that give solid proof of guilt. We're hoping Laila will give some since we are sure of her involvement. The question is whether we are dealing with an organized gang or with just a few individuals who are amateurs. Both elements seem to be mixed together, and this adds to the puzzle. However, we think we know one of the other persons who is tied in with Laila."

"Then if you can get her to give you proof, you may solve the whole thing."

Again Katie saw that quick exchange of looks between aunt and nephew. Andrew's voice was very serious when he answered. "You should know, Katie, that my aunt and I have discovered there is more to this than just the counterfeit scheme, serious as that is. That is the immediate problem, of course. But there is a personal aspect that has unexpectedly come to light. It is tied in with the fake money and yet is completely apart from that. We did not know about this other matter until Laila made a chance remark, one she did not know was so revealing because she doesn't know the whole story herself. But even the little knowledge she has puts her in danger of her life."

Katie, listening, wondered, *Was this what Mrs. Sieverson had meant by the words said in such a broken voice, "This gives a terrible new meaning to the problem"?*

Andrew went on, "Our guarding of the place where she is staying is partly for her protection, though she does not know that. Last night's vandalism here confirms our growing suspicions that there is more to this venture than appears on the surface. But we *cannot* see how the two separate pieces fit together."

He stopped, and then with seeming irrelevance he said, "Katie, about the mailman. We are sure someone was masquerading when he stopped you—deliberately masquerading, apparently."

"But why? Why a mailman? And why would he stop to talk instead of just hurrying by?"

Mrs. Sieverson answered, "You said when you

ied to describe him and couldn't that you did not
otice the person, but just the uniform."

"He wanted to come to the house without arous-
ıg suspicion, so he used the uniform as a dis-
uise," Andrew explained. "He either wanted to get
omething out of the mail box that Laila had left for
im, or put something in. We think it must have
•een that he wanted to get something and did not
ucceed and so made the desperate attempt to find
last night. As to why he stopped to talk to you?" He
hrugged, though his voice was grim. "It was sheer
onfidence in his ability to fool you."

"But who would it be that I would know? None of
aila's friends, certainly. It would have to be you or
Barry or Mark—"

That nagging memory of Mark sitting in his car
ate at night staring at the house came back. An-
lrew's words repeated themselves in her ears—"He
vas sure he could fool you."

She shook her head and looked from one to the
ther. "But what is it he wants?" adding to herself,
specially if it is Mark.

"Katie."

Andrew's voice was unsure, groping, and she
ooked at him. "I'm going to ask you to do some-
hing without giving you a reason for it or even an
xplanation. You have every right to refuse, because
. could be dangerous, and if you do we will not
•ress you on it. But it is a plan that could help solve
ıot only this puzzle but—"

He stopped, his eyes asking counsel of his aunt,
vho nodded her answer. He finished, "But it might

give answers to questions we have asked for years about another riddle."

"I'll do anything I can."

Mrs. Sieverson stood up then and went out of the room, and Katie heard her go upstairs. She came back with a notebook, which Andrew took from her and laid on the table between them.

"As you can see, this is the kind of notebook you have been using these weeks. I would like you to write clearly on the front cover, 'Notes from Mrs. Sieverson.' Then on the first page put 'Notes from Journal, 1900-1950.'"

He waited while she wrote. When she looked across at him, he said, "Now fill about thirty pages or so with your shorthand system."

"But what? What shall I write?—You mean, just put down anything?"

"If you are absolutely sure your code can't be broken, put down anything, whether it makes sense or not. Talk about the weather, or what you had for breakfast, or make a grocery list—anything, as long as it is in your scribbled code and no one but you can understand it."

He watched, and when she had filled about twenty pages, his hand moved to stop her. "Now keep on with several pages like that, but put a name in occasionally here and there. Put Lars in so that it can be plainly read."

She looked up, understanding coming. "This is to trap someone! Then should I put other names in? Yours? And Barry's? Maybe even Laila's?"

He nodded, his expression grave. He watched

her fill ten more pages before explaining, "Katie, we are asking you to carry this notebook quite openly for the next several days—at school, when you are in the downtown library, even if you go shopping. I know it seems like a foolish idea. And I don't know that anyone seeing it will question you. But if someone, *anyone*, should, say you are helping with my aunt's writing project—which is true, of course—but make it clear that you have not got very far, that you have not gone beyond 1950. Make that very clear."

His voice was so insistent that Katie nodded, though tension knotted her throat to keep back words.

Then Andrew asked, "You know about Lars, of course."

It was both a statement and a question, and she nodded. Again no words came. The pain on his face made her realize how hard this was for him, and for Mrs. Sieverson who sat with one hand shading her eyes. But it also made something clear to her.

"So whoever broke in last night probably was not looking either for counterfeit money or for valuables. He was looking for something else in here." Her eyes went to Mrs. Sieverson in startled certainty. "He wanted the letters and diaries you had in the small chest. He knew you kept them there." She frowned in dismay. "But that would have to be someone you know. Someone in the family—"

"Or someone Laila told because she knew about them," Andrew cut in quickly.

"I don't understand why they would be important. Do they tell about buried treasure from some an-

193

cestor? From one of the boats that broke up in lake storm?"

"I wish it were that simple." Again Andrew's voi carried so much pain that it stopped Katie's que tions.

The hours stretched endlessly across the mor ing. Laila remained in hiding, stubbornly silent b hind locked doors, refusing to talk to Mrs. Sieverso Andrew shook his head to suggestions that th police force her out. "No. She is safer there for th time being. Just keep a guard posted and report me if anyone tries to see her."

Katie could not settle down to study for test Instead, she helped bring a semblance of order the slashed room. She was appalled again at th viciousness with which the intruder had vented h rage. Deep scars gouged ugly wounds in what ha been a smooth, gleaming desk surface, leavin ragged splinters of wood.

"Whoever did this must have a savage, viole streak that goes wild when he doesn't get what h wants." Katie looked around as she spoke. Then she saw the cold, methodical destruction, sh shook her head, perplexed. "Still, this looks though it were done deliberately. As though the pe son had planned it out beforehand."

Mrs. Sieverson nodded agreement and reache to smooth the torn gold brocade upholstery wit fingers that trembled.

They both turned as Andrew came into the roon and Mrs. Sieverson hurried to him, holding out h hands protestingly.

"Andrew! It is not safe to go through with the notebook idea. All of this is proof of how dangerous the idea might be." She gestured around the room. "See what he did in here."

"She will be protected," he answered gently, taking her hands in his reassuringly. He turned to Katie. "Mr. Johnson is coming up the driveway. I am going to stand in the doorway and talk to him for a few minutes. Try to decide if he sounds like the man who spoke to you the other day."

Katie stood out of sight on the stair landing and listened. When Mr. Johnson turned away, Andrew beckoned her to watch him walk down the driveway. She shook her head in regret when Andrew closed the door.

"I just couldn't tell. There was a similarity in his general appearance, but I didn't pay enough attention the other time to his voice and mannerisms. I just couldn't say it was the same man—" She broke off and looked at him. "But I thought you said you knew it was not Mr. Johnson."

"I'm sure it wasn't. But I must know how closely the imposter looked and sounded like him. You would have thought it was this man?"

His voice was so strongly insistent that Katie stared back at him puzzled, wondering why it mattered, what difference the mailman made in the counterfeit scheme.

Finally she stammered, "I—I think so. Though probably those who know him would see a difference."

195

Andrew turned away without comment, but I aunt stopped him again.

"I still think we should let this go. It has been many years—I have lived with the hurt so long have given it to God. Andrew, why not let it rest cannot bear to have someone else in danger b cause of what happened so long ago in the past

Andrew stood irresolute, gnawing at his lip. The he walked over to the study door and looked aga at the shattered room. He turned back to face I aunt.

"We must go through with it." His voice was ge tle but definite. "*We* may want to forget it, push back in the mists of the past, but will the oth person? What has been dormant for all these yea has suddenly begun to grow, like a cancer. It has be cut out to stop it from doing more damage."

"But to bring Katie into it—"

"Katie is in it just by living here these weel Somehow she was brought into the counterfeit p for some whim we have yet to figure out. But havir lived here involves her in the other part of the pro lem. That's my fault, I know, and I am sorry. I've to her so." His look across at Katie made her feel as she were part of the family. "But there is no backir out now. He will think she knows more than sl does."

"Then we should tell her—warn her—"

Andrew shook his head in such a decisive motio that there was no room for further argument.

"No, it's better that she go into it innocently. I more dangerous, I know, but that's the only way tl

plan will succeed. If she knew everything we suspect, she would be too much on guard, would not
be able to act naturally. That might put her in real
danger at a time when we could not protect her."

Katie listened, looking from one to the other as
the conversation went back and forth. She felt like a
pawn on a chessboard, not able to make any moves
for herself, completely helpless in their grasp and in
the possible grasp of an implacable enemy—a
nameless, faceless enemy.

She only knew that, regardless of danger to herself, she would do anything to free Mrs. Sieverson
from the burden of hurtful memories she carried.

TWELVE

Katie wakened the next morning to the sparkling gloss of a clear, cold fall day. Breakfast smells came invitingly as she stretched and looked at the clock. She remembered the mysterious plan she was part of, and she sat up in bed to think about it, pulling the blanket up over her shoulders.

Today was Sunday. The hours would go slowly while they waited for the plan to develop. She frowned over it. What did Andrew expect would happen? She looked across the room at the little antique blue desk where the notebook sat safely in a drawer, waiting for her to carry it conspicuously tomorrow and for however many days were necessary while they waited for the unknown enemy to make another move. At least today she would be safe in the house. And yet—the thought of being alone all morning in the empty house was suddenly frightening.

Why not go to church with Mrs. Sieverson? She and Andrew would go as usual, regardless of their anxiety, because that was where they would leave some of their care. If she went too it would be one way to fill the long morning and perhaps, perhaps she would find answers to the questions that were intruding into the orderliness of her life. Any deepening friendship with Andrew would be impossible unless she found those answers—and could accept them.

She showered and dressed quickly, feeling strangely carefree, and ran lightly downstairs. The polished bannister slid smoothly under her hand. The dining room table was set as always with the best china, heavy silver, crystal goblets, and a fresh centerpiece of flowers. Very little could change the routine of a Sunday dinner that had been a part of Mrs. Sieverson's life since coming into the house as a young wife.

Katie stopped and looked at the beautifully set table. She thought of the shy young girl who had come from so barren a background into the elegance of this house. What a contrast it must have been to her. Yet, what a richness she had brought to this family of her own inner spiritual wealth. Katie wondered if her husband had known what a gem he had.

That train of thought brought the questions back. Until now her life had seemed rich and complete in love and books and mental stimulation. She had thought she needed nothing more until she found a man she could love. Now she was not sure. Had her parents cheated themselves and her, unknowingly, by leaving God out of their lives? The thought was shattering in its implications, for it meant she was criticizing the ones she had loved and respected all her life. She thrust the idea away as she turned suddenly from the beauty and charm of the table and pushed through the swinging doors into the kitchen.

Mrs. Sieverson looked up and smiled her greeting. Her hand held open the Bible beside her plate. "Good morning, Katie. Are you joining me for breakfast?"

"If I may," she answered, slipping into a place across the table and accepting the cup of fragrant coffee Mrs. Sieverson poured for her. She felt embarrassed showing this sudden interest in church after not having gone other weeks, and she did not want Mrs. Sieverson to attach too much importance to it. She asked quickly, to keep from changing her mind, "May I go with you to the service this morning?"

The quick, glad look came on Mrs. Sieverson's face, as she had known it would, and she added hastily in explanation, "I feel a little nervous about being alone in the house today."

"I will be glad of your company. Andrew has already gone to teach his class, but I decided to miss Sunday school and simply go to the service today. I had a little trouble sleeping last night."

Katie looked at her compassionately, seeing the deep shadows under her eyes and the droop to her usually erect, slender shoulders. But Mrs. Sieverson went on, the light still in her eyes, "Now I am glad that I was late in getting around this morning. It means having your company. If you can be ready in half an hour, that will give ample time."

When they went out to the car, Katie took a deep breath of the clear air. "This sun is incredible after yesterday's gloom. How can the weather change so suddenly?"

"It does it all the time," Mrs. Sieverson answered. "It is God's way of letting us know that He is still in control of the world. We might have thought at times yesterday that the sun was not even in the sky anymore. But, there it is."

The confident, joyful lilt of her voice filled the car as they drove along the quiet, winding streets past the trees, whose branches now were bare of their colorful leaves. Mrs. Sieverson's enthusiasm was in keeping with the sunshine that gilded the day and danced off the blue waves topped with whitecaps that would soon be ice.

The quiet of the church building rested Katie. She liked the comfortably padded seats, the beauty of the green and blue and gold windows, and the grandeur of the hymns, even though they were unfamiliar. The minister's voice was clear and resonant as he read selected verses from what he called, "Isaiah, the Old Testament song of God's salvation." She sat with her hands loosely clasped in her lap, listening to the quiet beauty and dignity of the words.

And a man shall be as an hiding place from the wind, and a covert from the tempest; as rivers of water in a dry place, as the shadow of a great rock in a weary land. . . . He shall feed his flock like a shepherd: he shall gather the lambs with his arm, and carry them in his bosom, and shall gently lead those that are with young. . . . they that wait upon the Lord shall renew their strength; they shall mount up with wings as eagles; they shall run, and not be weary; and they shall walk and not faint. . . . I will bring the blind by a way that they knew not; I will lead them in paths that they have not known: I will make darkness light before them, and crooked things straight. These things will I do unto them, and not forsake them.

It was a quiet service and yet a demanding one as the minister used the Bible to picture the almighty, sovereign God, who yet was compassionate and loving. It was the picture of Him Mrs. Sieverson had been painting over and over in the weeks Katie had known her, a picture she was finding hard to evade.

She had not expected to know anyone, but she recognized a few in the congregation who were fellow students. One of her professors sat two rows over, nodding his agreement of the minister's words. She had a glimpse of Barry sitting alone down near the organ, listening intently to the sermon and singing the hymns vigorously.

I wish I had nerve enough to ask Mrs. Sieverson more about his family, she thought idly. *Does his mother ever leave the house?* Barry's happy-go-lucky nature apparently had escaped the gloom of his mother's poor health.

Most of all, through the service she was aware of Andrew sitting on the other side of his aunt. He had come in just as the first hymn was announced and gave her a glad, welcoming smile. Though she tried to pay attention to all that was going on, she was acutely conscious of his presence, of his interest in the sermon, and of his easy familiarity in handling his Bible.

Barry saw her as she and Mrs. Sieverson came out of the church. He waved, his face showing recognition and surprise. He came over to them, his clear eyes smiling his greeting.

"Isn't this great weather after yesterday's gloom? How are you girls today?" He smiled from one to the other. "Katie, all that rain yesterday washed away any footprints of your mysterious prowler. I didn't see any evidence of him at all."

"Maybe *you* didn't, but—" Katie began but stopped to reach quickly for Mrs. Sieverson's purse which slid from her grasp as she unlocked the car door.

"I am sorry," Mrs. Sieverson exclaimed as Katie and Barry stooped to retrieve the items that had spilled out.

Barry held the car door for them and said, "Look, tell Laila I'm sorry I didn't call her yesterday as I had promised. Dad kept me busy in the office. Tell her I'll call this afternoon. Thanks."

Katie watched him walk to his car, feeling momentary regret that he had not offered her a ride. She slid in beside Mrs. Sieverson and said, "We should have told him she won't be home this afternoon. Do you think he suspects anything?"

"About what?" Mrs. Sieverson's voice was

abstracted as she watched the oncoming traffic before pulling out of the parking lot.

"About Laila. That she is in this mess with the counterfeiters. They *are* good friends, aren't they?"

"Oh." After a moment of concentrating on her driving, Mrs. Sieverson went on, "I do not know how involved he is with her, how close a relationship they have. They have dated in an on-again, off-again way ever since she came to live with us. But I do not know how much they really shared with each other of their hopes and dreams."

Katie glanced at Mrs. Sieverson's profile as she watched the street, driving carefully, her hands gripping the steering wheel tightly. She listened to Mrs. Sieverson's soft voice.

"Remember Laila's background, Katie, and do not judge her too harshly. When this is all over and she comes back—"

"You will take her back?"

"Of course. If she wants to come back. She has no other home, you see. She will have to bear whatever consequences the law demands, but that does not include losing a home with us."

Katie sat in silence as Mrs. Sieverson turned the car into the driveway and ran it in through the wide garage doors. *Forgiveness can be carried too far.*

The phone was ringing as they came into the warmth of the kitchen and Katie answered. It was Andrew.

"Katie, I'm sorry that I have been delayed and will not be home immediately. Please go ahead and eat

205

dinner without me. Tell my aunt not to try to keep anything warm, as I am not sure when I will be free."

After they had eaten, not talking much, each busy with her own thoughts, Mrs. Sieverson smiled across the flowers and crystal. Her face was lined with weariness.

"Forgive me, my dear, for deserting you for a little while. I simply must take a nap. I feel as though I could sleep for a week."

Katie nodded understandingly. "Please do. I'll clear up these things, and then I might lie down for a while too."

But when she had carefully washed and put away the beautiful heirloom dishes, she found herself too restless to lie down. Instead she got a book and curled up on the sofa in the living room, warm from the bright sunshine pouring in through the many windows. A light tapping roused her presently, and she looked up to see Barry outside the French doors that opened onto the patio at the side of the house. She went across and unlocked them.

"Has Laila forgiven me?" Barry stepped inside as he asked.

"She isn't here. She wasn't home for dinner."

"Oh. I thought she might take a walk with me. I'm really sorry I messed up yesterday's plans. But this is the kind of day she likes, and I hoped she would let me make it up to her."

He obviously did not know about Laila at all, and Katie stood, trying to sort out what to tell him. Since he was her friend, maybe he could help her if he knew the whole story. But she checked the words. It was ridiculous, of course, to be suspicious of Barry, but she had promised not to talk to anyone about what was going on. She hoped the study door was closed in case he decided to walk out and get something from the refrigerator. Better that he not see the destruction in the room and ask questions.

Barry stood smiling at her, his head cocked to one side, his hands on his hips. "Well, how about your coming with me? I know that sounds as though you are just a substitute for Laila, but I don't mean it that way." His smile flashed his apology, and Katie smiled back.

"Thanks, Barry, but I'm in an exciting part of a book, and I want to finish it this afternoon."

He looked down at the book she had left lying face down and leaned to pick it up. "Early Settlers of the Midwest"? His face and voice registered his incredulity. "Exciting?" he echoed.

Then he saw the notebook and picked it up. He looked at the first page and whistled softly. "This is quite a shorthand system you have." He riffled through the pages casually.

Then he looked across at her, admiration clear in his eyes. "Aunt Sigrid always had a knack for seeing under the surface of a person. But it beats me how she could look at you in the library and know immediately that you would share her interest in the history of this part of the country."

He looked at the book title again. "I hope the two of you will put your findings in a book and get it out of her system. She's been keeping every scrap of information in books and newspapers and letters since I was a kid."

He tossed the notebook down. "Well, it's a blow to my male ego that you would rather spend a beautiful, clear, sunny day with a history book than with me. But so be it."

He went back through the French doors, turned to wave, and loped off down the driveway. Katie watched him turn to jog along the street toward his house, and went impulsively to the French doors and pulled them open.

"Barry! Wait for me!"

But he had gone too far to hear her call, and she turned back inside, regretting a lost opportunity. Jane was right—she never gave anyone a chance to get acquainted. But Barry obviously was not interested in her. He had not tried to persuade her to come; he had not really cared.

She picked up the notebook and looked through it in the careless way he had done. She tried to see it through the eyes of someone who might be eager to know its secrets, or someone like Barry who was just idly curious about it. It did look mysterious and, yes, Lars's name did leap out suddenly. The only recognizable words were his name and the few times she had written Barry and Andrew.

She dropped the notebook on the couch and wandered restlessly around the room, thinking how different it looked to her now. When she had first come to the house, she had seen only the beautiful *things*, the wealth of the place. Now the spirit of the room, the house, and the family was taking hold of her. So many of her first impressions had been wrong. She had thought Mrs. Sieverson had been born to a life of wealth and ease, that that was what accounted for her poise and serenity. Instead it had been the poverty and tragedy of her life that had molded and shaped her and given her the courage to face the empty room upstairs and say, "I would not doubt God's wisdom."

Katie's mind circled the words as she stared unseeing at the blue of the lake beyond the sinister rocks. That was it. God had done it. Three weeks ago she had no thought of God. Now she could not escape Him anywhere in this house. And she was not altogether sure she wanted to.

She jumped when the phone rang and hurried to answer before the shrill sound could waken Mrs. Sieverson.

"Katie? Andrew. May I speak to my aunt?"

"She is sleeping. Shall I call her?"

"No, don't wake her. Katie—"

She strained to hear his voice above the crackle along the line, and said, "Can you speak louder? This connection is poor. I can't hear you very well."

"I can't hear you clearly either," he answered. "I'm calling from a pay phone and there is so much noise here. Katie, will you bring that notebook." He stopped, his voice guarded. "You know the one I mean. I don't want to mention on the phone—"

"Yes, yes. I know."

"Bring it and come down to the end of the street. You'll come to a big rock just after you circle around the curve and before you get very far along the shore. I don't know if you've ever been there to see it to know which one I mean."

"Yes, I was there with Barry once."

"Well, don't go past that rock. Wait for me there. And, Katie, be very careful. If you see or hear anything suspicious on your way there or while you are waiting for me, run home. Hear me?"

"Yes, I'll be careful."

"If my aunt is awake, tell her you are meeting me so she won't worry, but don't tell her where, or she will worry anyway. Come right away."

The crackling and the noise on the line stopped as the connection was broken.

Katie put down the receiver, snatched up the notebook, and ran upstairs for a thick sweater. She stopped outside Mrs. Sieverson's door and tapped lightly, glad when there was no answer. She needed a long, sound sleep to erase the worn look she had had at dinner.

She went downstairs quickly and let herself out the front door. As it closed quietly behind her, she heard the click of the automatic lock. No one could get in now unless Mrs. Sieverson let him in. And she was safe because she would open the door only to someone she knew and trusted.

She walked quickly along the street, thinking how quiet Sunday afternoons were in this part of town. In Mrs. Ireland's neighborhood, children shrieked constantly, their play sounding like battles. Here, no young children were out playing in the bright sunshine. Some of the houses were already closed up for the winter, the owners gone south.

It was at least a ten-minute walk to the rock Andrew had mentioned. She had to go all the way to the end of the street and then circle along the shore following the pavement. Apparently years earlier, the city planners had expected more people to build homes along that stretch of land and had laid out a sidewalk. But no one had come to that spot, and the sidewalk was overgrown with weeds and beginning to crumble at places where the water washed up over it.

Katie reached the big rock and leaned against it. Her breath came quickly from her fast walk. She looked out over the lake and could understand why no one had wanted to build down here so close to the water. The roar of the waves was bad enough high up on the brow of the hill where the Sieverson and Jorgenson houses stood. Down here it would be deafening, and winter gales would shake a house unmercifully. Even the cliff behind it would not give enough protection from blasts of wind. And the desolateness of this stretch of shore, the whole length of it, would be difficult to endure day after day. She shivered and pulled her sweater collar up, wondering how children could have enjoyed playing here. Perhaps because they were children, they were unaffected by the mood, and did not see danger lurking behind every monstrous rock.

The minister had read about a hiding place from the wind and of a great rock being a shadow that offered security. That did not describe this place, for here the wind was an enemy and the rocks were threatening.

A step behind her made her straighten up and turn around eagerly to meet Andrew. But it was Barry who stood there, smiling at her. She stood motionless, the eagerness fading from her face.

The expression in his eyes told her how foolish she had been to come out of the house without anyone's knowing where she was. How foolish not to have guessed it was Barry behind all that was happening. There was no comfort in the thought that Andrew knew where she was, that he had told her to meet him there, that he would soon come, because he might not get to her in time. The smile on Barry's lips let her know as plainly as though he had spoken the words aloud that he had no mercy for anyone who thwarted him.

"I'll take that notebook, Katie," he said, his voice easy and friendly.

THIRTEEN

She faced him and forced herself to smile and shrug carelessly. "There's nothing in it, Barry. Nothing that makes sense, I mean. It's just a lot of my silly scribbling. You know—you already saw it. You see, long ago my father and I invented a silly shorthand method when I was little, just for fun. I use it to take notes in class. And—and I have to keep practicing it so I won't forget it. This is a notebook full of—of just nothing."

If only he knew how true that is, she thought as she heard her voice babbling her response.

But he moved toward her slowly, his eyes steady on her, cold, without a shred of pity. "With my name—and Lars—and Andrew sprinkled all through it? I saw the names. You got the story from Mrs. Sieverson. You know things from the past."

She laughed unsteadily and tried to keep her voice light. "Oh, Barry, I put those names in just for fun. I—I wanted to see which one I liked the best. They are the only words in the notebook that mean anything, that make sense. The rest is just nonsense."

213

She took a few uncertain steps backward, trying to keep away from him and yet not get too far from the big rock before Andrew came. She discarded the impulse of trying to circle around him and make a run back to the street. He could easily outrun her. But if she kept his back to the rock, he would not see Andrew coming until it was too late. Somehow she would try to signal Andrew that Barry was the one they wanted.

But then she realized Barry was forcing her along the shore step by slow step. And he was keeping her in the shadow of the cliff away from the open shore where someone might look down from above and see them. They were so close to the side of the cliff that the sun did not reach the dark rock, and the cold wind bit through the sweater. But fright chilled her more than the wind.

As he moved inexorably toward her, she panicked. "Andrew will be here any minute. He knows I'm here. He called and told me to meet him here, so you had better leave while you can."

She stopped as a cruel smile twisted his mouth, changing his face from friendly charm to something evil.

The truth caught her. "It was you, not Andrew who called! I thought it was his voice, but it sounded different. It was the noise, the crackling on the line that made it sound strange. But it was you!"

He shrugged, his voice and manner still light and casual. "There are lots of ways to disguise a voice just enough to fool poor innocent people."

"Then—you were the mailman! You disguised

214

yourself—your voice—pulled your cap down low. You put on a false mustache."

He stood still, his smile mocking her exclamations. Then he assumed Mr. Johnson's slightly hunched shoulders and squinted at her. "I hope I've left you some good mail," he said, his voice mumbling as though he talked around a mouthful of something. The mocking smile returned as he said, "That wasn't the only time you saw me and didn't know it."

She stared back at him and the little pieces that had nudged her memory other times fell in place. "Your mustache the first time I saw you was false," she cried with certainty. Then she added, "You must have been in the library other times I was there and I didn't see you, didn't recognize you. But why?"

He laughed at her but with no softening in his face and eyes as he said, "Give me the notebook first, and then I'll answer your questions."

Hope drained away as she stared at the hardness of his face. Andrew didn't know she was here. No one knew. The only thing she could do to save herself was try to convince him that the notebook was harmless, that it held no secrets about him or the past.

He was gradually forcing her farther and farther along the shore away from the street and toward the huge rocks just below the Sieverson house. She heard the waves pounding the rocks, not a soothing, washing and lapping sound, but a crashing snarl. She tried to think and plan some way to make him believe that she knew nothing about any secret.

215

Her mind scrabbled back through events Mr
Sieverson had mentioned, events Barry might hav
been connected with. Another thought came the
but she tried to thrust it away. Some child—a frien
of Lars and of Barry—had almost drowned. An
Lars had been pulled under— Could Barry hav
done—? Was that the secret? No! It was too impos
sible, too monstrous even to think of.

She gave the water only a quick glance, not da
ing to take her eyes long off Barry. She must kee
away from it, not let him force her so close to th
edge.

"Are you going to give me that notebook, Katie
You know I don't want to hurt you." He took on
slow step after another, forcing her to retreat.

"I tell you there is nothing in it."

With his eyes steady on hers, she saw him reac
into his jacket pocket and pull out a small gree
diary with a clasp lock.

"Where did you get that? Mrs. Sieverson keeps
in her room." Fright seized her. "You were in th
house! But—how did you get in?" She could hea
again the lock clicking when she had closed th
door, shutting Mrs. Sieverson in to safety. In he
hurry to obey instructions she thought came fror
Andrew, she had forgotten that someone else had
key to the house, and she had actually locked Mr
Sieverson into danger.

Barry was answering her. "You forget I've been i
and out of that house all my life. It's like a secon
home. I've always had a key. I thought old stodg
Andy would have guessed that. I have keys to all th

216

houses around here," he finished with a careless shrug.

"Mrs. Sieverson would never have given you that diary willingly. What did you do to her?"

He shrugged with that same carelessness. "Tied her up." Then his voice hardened. "Now let's cut out this run-around. I want that notebook. I'm going to destroy it and this diary. When I do, there will be nothing to connect me with what happened that day. I was a kid. It was a kid game, nothing more. Things just went wrong, that's all. There's no need for anyone to keep bringing up what should be dead and buried and forgotten." He held out his hand.

"I tell you there is nothing about the past in this notebook. There are no secrets of any kind in it."

"Then there is no reason why you can't give it to me."

Katie clutched it against her, holding the thin cardboard covers tightly. He was right—it would not matter. Except that she instinctively knew she was safe only as long as she had the notebook. So she stubbornly shook her head, keeping just beyond his reaching hands.

His face darkened. "Give it to me so you can get back to dear Aunt Sigrid in time. I turned on the heater in her room but neglected to light the gas. If she isn't found soon, some people will say, 'Poor old thing. How could she have been so careless?'"

Katie threw the notebook at him. "Take it!"

She circled around to dart past him, but Barry lunged at her and caught her wrist in a hard grip.

"Oh, no, you don't. It's not that simple any longer.

217

I have to take care of both you and Aunt Sigrid otherwise you will talk. I can't trust her to keep silent any longer. And now you know too much."

He began to pull her along the shore, away from the rocks and toward the angry water. Katie tried to dig her heels in the sand, protesting, "Barry, don't do anything more! You can't expect to get away with this."

She saw his face and knew her protests were futile. How had she ever thought him charming and fun to be with? His fingers dug into her arm as he dragged her after him along the hard ground.

"Barry! Stop!" Katie heard the shout from Andrew as he came around the big rock and ran toward them.

Barry looked back over his shoulder and then pushed her to the ground. Then he turned and raced along the shore in the opposite direction, tearing sheets out of the notebook and shredding them into the wind. Andrew came running and stooped over, helping her up.

"Are you all right?" His eyes were anxious as he looked at her.

She nodded, half crying with relief, and exclaimed, "Andrew! Barry said—"

He cut her off impatiently. "Not now! Tell me later." He turned and ran again, but he had only gone a few yards when he stopped and looked around. Katie caught up with him as he exclaimed, "Where did he go? I only had my eyes off him long enough to help you up, but he has disappeared. He must be

218

hiding behind those rocks down there along the cliff at the other end."

But Katie was crying, tugging frantically at his arm. "Andrew! Listen to me! Your aunt. We have to get to her. Barry said he tied her up in her bedroom and turned on the gas heater. But it isn't lighted! He did it on purpose!"

His face darkening with anger, Andrew turned her around, his hands rough on her shoulders, and grabbed her hand. "Come on!" He pulled her as she stumbled along over the uneven ground, until they got to the end of the shore where the sidewalk began. Then he turned her loose and ran, throwing words over his shoulder.

"I'll go ahead. You'll be safe here, but hurry." His long stride carried him quickly up the street out of her sight.

Katie ran too, her breath coming in hard gasps and her throat aching from swallowing the cold air. By the time she got to the house and hurried up the stairs, Mrs. Sieverson lay stretched out on her bed. Andrew had flung the windows wide to the reviving chill of the air and was bending over his aunt, holding her hands tenderly.

As Katie hovered near the foot of the bed, not daring to ask if they had reached her in time, Mrs. Sieverson's eyelids fluttered and lifted slowly. Looking around, she struggled to sit up.

"Lie still." Andrew's hands were gentle as he pushed her down against the pillows.

"Katie," she whispered.

"Katie is all right. Everything is fine."

"But Barry—Katie—" The wisp of voice trailed off.

"Katie is right here. She's all right. The police will find Barry. Just rest and don't think about it."

"He—took—my diary. Said he—would hurt Katie—if I refused."

"I know. We'll get it back. We'll find him. Aunt Sigrid, I've called the doctor. After he looks at you and things are quiet, we'll have a long talk. Just the three of us." He looked around over his shoulder at Katie, his smile gathering her into the circle of three.

The doctor came immediately, and Andrew let him in, explaining the need tersely before he took him upstairs, not naming names but speaking only of "an intruder." While the doctor examined Mrs. Sieverson, joshing her affectionately, Katie fixed soup and sandwiches and fruit and coffee.

The doctor came downstairs, speaking briefly to Andrew in the hall.

"She has had a shock, but fortunately her heart is strong. She will be all right. Try to keep her from doing too much for the next day or so." He looked at Andrew. "You don't want anything said about this, I suppose? You don't think the police should be notified in case of further danger?"

"They are already in on it," Andrew answered.

The doctor did not ask questions as he shrugged himself into his coat. "I've taken care of this family for so long, you're like part of my own. I don't understand why anyone would want to harm Sigrid Sieverson. It would take a twisted mind to do a thing like this deliberately."

220

"I'm afraid that's exactly what we have here."

Katie heard the bleakness in Andrew's voice as he answered and then opened the door, his hand reaching to grip the doctor's hand.

"Thanks for coming so quickly. We'll call tomorrow to let you know how she is getting along."

The doctor stood on the wide front steps and turned again to Andrew. Katie could hear the low, hesitant tone as he asked, "Do any of you ever see Mrs. Jorgenson?"

"No."

Andrew's voice was curt, but the doctor did not seem to notice as he turned away, shaking his head. "Someone needs to get into that house and persuade her to live again. She absolutely refuses to see me."

Andrew closed the door and turned to Katie. "I'll bring my aunt down away from her room for a while. Let me put a table close to the windows over there at the end of the living room and we can eat our supper there."

He carried his aunt down to a big easy chair, while Katie brought in the trays of dishes and food. They left the draperies wide open so they could see the sun setting over the lake, streaking crimson and gold and gray lines of color on the distant horizon where the sky and water met.

Katie looked anxiously at Mrs. Sieverson's white, tired-looking face. She felt remorse at having unwittingly caused what could have been tragedy. Her voice was contrite as she said, "I'm so sorry to have put you through all this. If I had just stayed here, Barry could not have gotten at you."

"He would have found some other way," Mrs. Sieverson comforted her.

"You mustn't blame yourself," Andrew agreed. "Once he saw the notebook nothing would stop him. He was determined to have it." He checked his words abruptly and then asked, "When *did* he see it?"

"He was here this afternoon, looking for Laila. Then as we talked, he just picked it up and sort of glanced through it. I had no idea he was behind all this." Katie stopped, shaken by the thought of how trusting she had been of him.

She looked at Andrew, wanting him to understand why she had gone to meet Barry. "He did sound like you on the phone, otherwise I would never have gone."

She thought back over the conversation, and explained, "It wasn't that his voice sounded like yours, because it wasn't very clear. It was *what* he said that was so convincing and made me think it was you. He said I should let Mrs. Sieverson know where I was going if she was awake. He asked if I knew where the big rock was. Well, he knew I had been there, but you didn't, so of course I didn't think it was Barry talking. And then he pretended to be so worried about my safety—he said I should turn and run if I saw anything suspicious."

She stopped, looking at Andrew gratefully. "If you had not come when you did—" She drew a deep, trembling breath as the memory of Barry's ruthlessness flooded back. Had Andrew been ten minutes later and Barry had disappeared, there would have been no way to prove that she had not accidentally drowned. There were no witnesses to the scene on the shore or to the careless turning on of a gas heater by an old lady in a closed bedroom.

"We can both be grateful to God that He sent Andrew home in time." Mrs. Sieverson's soft voice brought Katie back to the safety of the room.

"And that He sent your friends along. If it hadn't been for them, I might have been too late."

"My friends?" she repeated, not understanding. Then, "You mean Jane and Mark? They were here?"

He nodded. "They were driving along the street on the far side of Barry's house just opposite the tennis court, and they saw you come out and start down the street. They were going to follow you to be sure you were all right. But then they saw Barry—"

"Coming out of the house after he had been— upstairs?" She gave a quick, appealing look at Mrs. Sieverson, who was sitting relaxed in the depths of the big chair.

"No," Andrew said, "apparently he had been here and then gone back home. He came from his house, and they thought he was hurrying to catch up with you. They knew you would be safe with him." He stopped and looked at her with a faint smile. "I gather you had talked to them about him."

His voice held a question, and Katie nodded, not answering, as she remembered her description of Barry to them—charming, happy-go-lucky, friendly.

223

How blind she had been not to have seen below the surface charm!

"They had decided to go home when they saw me pull into the driveway. Just on impulse Mark called to me and told me you were out walking and what direction you had gone. When he mentioned Barry, I ran to get you. Of course they knew nothing of what had already gone on in here, so I did not come in. My only thought was to save you."

A protective note was clear in his voice, and Katie, hearing it, could only smile her gratitude. *Perhaps later I can trust myself to find words to thank him. Now I would only break down in tears.*

As she fought for control, she puzzled over Jane and Mark. "How did they happen to be here this afternoon? This is the third or fourth time in the last week that they have just sat out in Mark's car watching the house. Once it was late at night."

"I didn't take time for conversation. I just ran. You probably should call and tell them you are safe. They were genuinely concerned about you."

Andrew carried the trays back to the kitchen while Katie went to the study to dial Mrs. Ireland's number. Listening to the telephone ring, she looked around the room. She could easily imagine Barry slashing the chairs and tearing papers with that hard look in his eyes and the smile twisting his lips, enjoying the destruction. But far worse than this was the casualness with which he had dismissed her death and Mrs. Sieverson's as necessary. She closed her eyes to shut sight and memory away.

Mrs. Ireland's brusque, "Well who is it?" jerked her back.

"May I speak to Jane, please?"

She could hear the receiver clatter on the little table in the narrow hall and Mrs. Ireland clump to the foot of the stairs and call, "Jane! Phone."

A rush of feet on the stairs came immediately and Jane's breathless, "Katie?"

"How did you know I was calling?"

"I didn't. I only hoped. Mark just left so I knew it wasn't he. *What* is going on out there?"

"Too much to tell you right now. But I wanted you to know I am all right and to thank you for being there this afternoon."

"Listen, I've got dozens of questions to ask you—"

"And I've got some to ask you too about your mysterious actions."

"*My* mysterious actions! With policemen coming around to ask me about you?" Jane's voice was punctuated with exclamations. "Mark and I have really been worried about you."

"Jane, can you and Mark come out tomorrow afternoon? I may not make it to class tomorrow at all. But if you come, I'll tell you the whole story—and give Mark a chance to see the inside of the house," she added. Laughter was clear in her voice.

"We'll be there. But are you sure we don't have to come out and guard you anymore? Mark's car is beginning to turn that way automatically."

"No, the danger is over," she answered.

But as she put the receiver down and walked back

to the lamp-lit glow of the living room, she knew that the reasons for the danger were still unexplained. Her questions showed on her face as she sat down, and Mrs. Sieverson looked across at her. "I think you had better tell Katie the story from the beginning, Andrew."

Katie listened to Andrew tell it, and it was just as she had read it in the few diaries and letters Mrs. Sieverson had shown her. She heard again the stories of the cousins and numerous friends eagerly anticipating summer vacations at the Sieverson and Jorgenson homes set high on the cliff, with the length of the shore their sandbox and the whole lake their swimming pool.

But there were things Katie had not sensed as she had read the letters. There were quarrelings and suspicions. Occasionally a family came for a visit once and then the friendship cooled inexplicably and they never returned. Then came the summer Lars's friend had almost drowned. He had come back from the water, choking and gasping for breath, looking at Andrew with frightened eyes. The family had made veiled charges about Andrew to his parents and had never come back to visit.

"You mean—they thought *you* had tried to—to harm him?"

Andrew nodded his answer to Katie's question.

"But why? Why did they suspect you?"

"The boy said someone had suddenly grabbed him under the water from behind and tried to pull him down. He insisted a voice—my voice— whispered something about getting even. In his

226

frantic clutching to get away, he yanked off a fancy emblem the other boy was wearing on his trunks. It was mine, a commemorative thing my folks had brought me from Sweden earlier that year. Everyone knew it was mine. Apparently someone had 'borrowed' it."

"Barry? To throw suspicion on you? But why?"

"He was angry," was Andrew's brief, grim answer. "That summer he had done more than the usual number of his mean little tricks on people, and I had told him off about them. He got even with me by lashing out at someone younger and smaller than he."

She remembered Barry's voice as they had stood in the chill dusk and he had reminisced with laughing regret at being scolded for sprinkling sand over cinnamon rolls. After that the friend had almost drowned. Mrs. Sieverson had said it was a sequel.

Then she remembered something else. "When we talked that day about someone pretending to be the mailman, it reminded you of that, of someone pretending to be Andrew?"

Mrs. Sieverson nodded, her face ashen as memories rolled back the time. "Yes, and of other similar incidents. Things happened that no one could understand."

Katie said slowly, "I overheard you tell Andrew on the phone that the idea of a pretend mailman put a terrible new meaning on what was happening."

"Yes. It was then we were sure that Barry was at the heart of what was going on."

"Then came the winter Lars drowned." Andrew's

227

voice was somber as he told the story. Once again Katie imagined she could see the blinding sunshine of that winter day. The cold the week before had been so intense that the snow crunched underfoot, and people talked of little but the weather and of the zero records that were broken. Then, unexpectedly, had come several days of January thaw, and the temperature had soared from a bitter thirty below to an incredible fifty above.

All the children had been severely warned against trusting the ice to skate, especially the area where the sun reflected against an expanse of rock and kept the ice around and in front of it softer than along the rest of the shore.

There Lars had broken through. Though he frantically called for help as he hung onto the jagged ice that broke under his clutching grasp, no one could reach him in time. His last words, clearly heard across the breaking ice and the cries of the other boys were, "Barry—behind." That was all.

Andrew's voice was carefully controlled as he finished the story, making Katie realize how hard the telling of it was.

"No one could understand or explain how it had happened. Lars was unusually careful about skating. He always heeded advice about thin ice, or in summer dangerous water. How he could have been careless that day in the face of repeated adult warnings, no one could understand."

Katie finally asked the question. "How does Barry fit into all this?" suspecting the answer even before it came.

Her eyes shadowed and darkly blue, Mrs. Sieverson took from a pocket of her dressing gown a page cut from a diary. She handed it to Katie. It was dated February 14, 1952.

"This is the 'evidence' Barry thought he would find when he ransacked the house. It is all there is."

> Today is Valentine's Day, Lars' birthday, his twelfth. I write this with a heavy heart because he is gone, has been gone for three weeks. Yet I write with joy and hope because I know I will see him again. Since I believe that Jesus died and rose again, I believe "them also which sleep in Jesus"—Lars—"will God bring with Him."

> Now I must live with only the memory of a precious life taken needlessly—and with the constant sight of the one who did it. I did not see it happen, and yet I know Barry is responsible. He did it from the blind rage that fills him when he is opposed.

> I wonder if he knows I suspect him. He comes over as he has always done for cookies. He smiles at me with his engaging smile and says how much he misses Lars.

> What shall I do? I cannot accuse him. I cannot risk spoiling his life. And there is his mother—my friend. What would it do to her?

> Dear God! Help me to forgive him and love him!

Katie read the page, the ink faded from long ago years, and looked up, her own eyes wet. "Didn't anybody see it happen?"

Andrew shook his head. "No one was there. The

rest of us were way down along the shoreline where the ice was thick almost to the bottom of the lake, it seemed. Lars and Barry were together. Then, all at once, we heard Lars call—"

Andrew stopped, swallowed hard, his jaw muscles tensing as he fought for control. "We all ran, but we couldn't get to him in time. We stretched out on the ice on our stomachs in a chain trying to reach him. But his heavy clothes dragged him under in spite of his clutching at the edges of the ice. There were just those words, and we didn't know what they meant. Since Barry was nowhere in sight, we assumed he had gone under too, that perhaps Lars was trying to save him. One of the boys ran for help and brought back some men who were going by on the street. They began groping for both bodies."

"By this time the fire department had arrived," Mrs. Sieverson's quiet voice interjected. "They brought equipment to aid the search."

Where were you? Katie wondered. *Standing there, watching? Hoping the God you believe in would do a miracle?* She could feel the tears spilling over as she listened to Andrew.

"Then Barry came walking along the shore. He started to run when he saw the firemen and the rest of us huddled around the black hole where the ice was broken. He had gone to play with another friend a couple of blocks away, he said, thinking Lars was perfectly safe."

Andrew stopped again, the frown deep on his face, as he burst out, "And he must not have been there. If he had been with Lars when the ice broke, when Lars called, he could not possibly have gotten out of sight without our seeing him. If he had come our direction, he would have passed us. In the other direction he would have had to run for miles before the cliff slopes enough to be accessible. We would have seen him. And none of us thought he would deliberately go off and leave Lars there in trouble. Barry was always—"

Andrew hesitated, and then went on slowly, "He was never a favorite of any of us. He was always playing practical jokes that were mean, that hurt and left scars. He was a bully who blubbered and ran home when jokes were played on him. But to go off and leave Lars like that would have been—"

He broke off abruptly, not saying the word, but it hung heavy in the air between them.

"We were not alone in our sorrow," Mrs. Sieverson said slowly, her eyes seeing far-off events. "It left a mark on Barry's mother."

"Yes, it had a devastating effect on her," Andrew said. "She had been very fond of Lars, sometimes it seemed she was closer to him than to her own son. She was a very nervous, emotional person, easily excited. The tragedy began to make an invalid out of her. Mr. Jorgenson's business took him away from home a good deal at that time, leaving her alone to raise Barry. She found it easy to give in to him. After Lars's death she gradually began to avoid seeing people and finally stopped altogether. She hasn't left the house at all in recent years. She even refuses to see Aunt Sigrid."

"Did she suspect Barry?"

Mrs. Sieverson shook her head. "I do not know, but through the years I have wondered." Her voice infinitely sad, she added, "I lost both my son and my friend at the same time."

"Barry told me she was an invalid and that was why he was over here so much as a child. He said he thought of you as his second mother."

They sat in silence, spent with emotion from reliving the past. Katie thought of the way Barry had spoken to her of Mrs. Sieverson, his voice full of affection and pity and compassion. Then she remembered the coarse, careless roughness of his words, "I tied her up" and "I turned on the heater but neglected to light the gas." The enormity of the crime and of his years of duplicity hit her. "How *could* you go on treating him as though nothing had happened?"

"How can I now, at this distance, tell you my feelings? Time has blurred the edges of the pain. At the time, I had no proof that what had happened was not an accident. I had only a glimmering sense of something not quite right in a child, a child of a beloved friend. Damaging hers would not bring mine back."

Katie could see that Mrs. Sieverson struggled to control her trembling voice as she admitted, "I did not find it easy to understand why I should first lose my husband while Lars was a small child and then Lars. There were many long, empty, dreary days and many sleepless nights before acceptance came. Later, much later, I could say with Job, that great man of long ago who lost all his possessions

232

nd family, 'Shall I receive only good at the hand of iod, and not evil?' "

She held up a quieting hand at Katie's sound of rotest. "No, no! That is not to blame God. But I had) believe it was a part of His design, even though I light never see the reason for the pattern."

Andrew spoke again. "I'm sure the Jorgensons now nothing about these activities Barry has been ito. He is so clever at fooling people." He looked at is aunt, his eyes dark with sorrow and regret. What will *this* do to her?"

"It may well be too heavy a blow for her to endure. Vhen we know for sure where Barry is—if the police ace him, I will go across and see if Inga will let me ı."

"Inga!" Katie repeated. "But—that was the name f your friend! It was her brother you married? That neans you really *are* Barry's aunt. I know he called ou that, but I thought it was just his friendly way." he looked at Andrew. "Then you all were cousins."

"Cousins but not friends."

Andrew stood up abruptly as he spoke and then :aned to gather his aunt from the chair. "Obviously Barry discovered some way up that cliff that the rest f us know nothing about. We'll look in the morn- ıg."

FOURTEEN

Katie awoke in the morning feeling rested, though her arm ached from Barry's bruising grip. She got up quickly to shower and dress, not wanting to delay whatever answers the day would bring. The house had an empty feeling as she went downstairs. The hall mirrors reflected her movements as she buttoned the cuffs of her pink and gold blouse. But it was not the threatening silence she had felt other days. Instead she was gathered into the security of the quiet elegance of the living room as she passed it, the reassuring deep tone of the grandfather clock in the hall, the polished warmth of the dining room, and the blaze of the sunlit kitchen. Her place was set for breakfast at the round table. A note lay in the center of the blue and yellow fringed tablecloth.

"Katie, Andrew has business with the police. I have gone along, hoping to see Laila. When we come back we will go down along the shore to see what we can discover."

She poured coffee and took it in to stand by the

living room window and look down again upon the deserted shore where Barry had tried to silence her, not knowing that such drastic action was not necessary. As he ran from Andrew he had flung the torn pages of the notebook to the wind, thinking he was disposing forever of something incriminating. Had he now discovered too that the diary was empty of evidence and that all his plotting had been needless?

She turned enough to see the shuttered windows of his house. They must hide the rooms where Mrs. Jorgenson spent her days, shut away and alone. What would she do when she discovered the truth about Barry? How could he possibly hide his actions this time?

The question was answered when Andrew returned, shaking his head as she asked it. "There is no trace of him. I'm afraid he has made a clean escape."

"Does that mean Laila will have to take all the blame for the counterfeit scheme?"

Mrs. Sieverson answered, her voice reflecting her happiness. "Katie, such good news! Laila has told us and the police all she knows about the whole affair, including Barry's coercion of her. Apparently he had terrified her in some way so that she was afraid of him. Oh, I know her fear of him did not show on the surface," she answered the doubt on Katie's face. "She should have come to us for help, but she was afraid even to do that."

Andrew interrupted, shaking his head. "If she had known Barry was afraid too, afraid of his past being

236

evealed, she might have told us what he was doing to her."

Mrs. Sieverson's eyes were bright and her voice confident as she said contentedly, "I feared that she was lost to us. But now she is coming back, a softer, more reachable person."

Remembering Laila's sullen arrogance, Katie turned away to hide her skepticism of such a quick change, and ran upstairs to get a warm coat.

When she came down, Andrew asked, "You don't mind missing classes today? The police may come a little later this morning and might need a description of what happened yesterday, what Barry said to you."

"No. I can get notes from someone." She followed Mrs. Sieverson out the heavy front door, and added, "I don't believe I could sit in class and listen to a professor lecture on Mexican history, when something like this is happening right here."

They walked silently along the quiet street and skirted the big rock where she had waited so confidently for Andrew. He led the way along the hard ground, keeping close to the cliff. He stopped now and then to look up the side of the rock and run his hands along the surface, which was smooth in places, rough in others. They walked slowly all the way along the shore, past the Sieverson house and then past the Jorgenson portion of the cliff. Then they turned and came back. Andrew walked back to stand at the water's edge and look up at the height, searching it with his eyes.

"There is *some* way up there. There has to be. I

237

know Barry used some way to escape yesterday or he couldn't have gotten out of my sight. And he must have known about it when we were kids."

"He might have hidden further along the shore behind those rocks." Katie pointed at them as she spoke. "Then when we left, he came out and just got away."

Andrew shook his head. "I didn't have my eyes off him long enough for him to have gone that far."

"Behind," Mrs. Sieverson said. "Lars said 'behind', Andrew. What would that mean?"

Andrew gnawed at his lip without answering as he surveyed the rocks again, hands in jacket pockets, eyebrows pulled together in a frown as he tried to see what was not there. He walked over to the cliff again, feeling its surface as he moved slowly along, stepping carefully over the uneven ground.

Mrs. Sieverson sat down on a boulder at the edge of the gray water, her coat collar turned up against the chill of the air and her hands burrowed deep in the full sleeves of her blue coat.

Katie followed Andrew, running her hands over the smooth wall of stone as he did. She stumbled over a loose rock, twisted her ankle, and sat down abruptly, her hands reaching out to break her fall. As she pushed against the sand, her fingers closed around a piece of cloth, and she looked at it, frowning at the familiarity of the smooth suede material.

"Andrew!" She looked up at him. "This is from Barry's jacket! I'm sure of it."

Andrew leaned over and took it from her and

238

turned to show it to his aunt. "From the jacket he was wearing yesterday?"

"Yes."

"It looks like the pocket." Mrs. Sieverson turned it over in her fingers as she spoke.

Andrew nodded. "I knew he had not had time to run the length of the shore before he disappeared. He was right here, right at this spot, and then somehow he got away. But how?"

He reached out to run his hands down the edge of an outcropping of rock. Then he moved closer to inspect it and said, "There is a narrow opening here that a person could squeeze through if there were anywhere to go. But surely the cliff is solid rock—"

"Wait! Don't move." Katie reached for the object that glinted in the sand as it shifted under Andrew's foot. "It's a flashlight. It must have been in Barry's pocket. I could tell the way the pocket hung down that something heavy was in it. I—I thought it might have been a gun."

"He must have caught his pocket on something which tore it off and the flashlight fell out. If he noticed it, he was too rushed to stop and pick it up."

Andrew snapped the flashlight on and ran the light along the protruding rock. He peered in through the narrow opening. "There *has* to be an open space in there, even though it's so dark I can't see in."

He reached his arm in and then looked back at them, nodding his head. "I'm moving my hand back and forth and can't touch anything on either side. I'm going to squeeze through."

They watched him crouch down and inch his way between the slabs of thick rock. They heard his voice reverberating with a hollow sound.

"It's like a small cave in here between the outer cliff and the hillside. And there are steps cut into the side of the hill. As far as I can tell, they go all the way to the top."

He squeezed back out and flashed the light for Katie as she knelt down and looked in through the opening.

Mrs. Sieverson caught her breath suddenly and said, "That explains a line in the diary of that first wife. It is a sentence I have puzzled over. She said, 'My Andrew can walk straight up the cliff, but no one is to know.' I thought it only wifely pride in her man's physical strength, that he perhaps came up hand over hand by a rope, and wondered why he would not be seen. But this—"

She gestured and then added, "But still—I do not understand how it could have remained a secret ever since."

"If others knew about it, it would have defeated its purpose," Andrew answered. "Undoubtedly it was intended as a stairway to safety because the country around here was so wild. The house was built where it was for protection, which was all right if you were at the top of the cliff. But a person could get trapped down here and need to get away in a hurry. For years there was continual trouble with Indians. The Sioux especially had a lot to revenge white settlers for in this whole area. One white person would be like any other to them."

Andrew turned to look at the water lapping the shore and added soberly, "The lake took its vengeance too, which meant wrecked cargo ships. You could easily get loot up the cliff if there were steps cut into it, steps only you knew about. As I remember, that Andrew Sieverson was not an ancestor I can be proud of."

His face was grave as he bent over to flash the light into the opening. "Funny, with all us kids playing around here constantly and yet we never discovered this secret place."

"Barry did." Mrs. Sieverson's grieving voice spoke. "And Lars at some time must have caught Barry—"

"Up to some deviltry," Andrew finished grimly. "And Barry's hot temper did its work. It may not have been deliberately planned. He may not have meant to let it get out of hand as it did. He may have thought someone would get to Lars in time."

"I must believe that." Mrs. Sieverson's soft voice was insistent. "I will go on believing that in the final sense it was an accident."

But Katie's memory flashed the picture of the destruction in the study, the deliberate, methodical, savage destruction. The same mind had planned both actions, the second done by the man grown from the child.

Words burst out. "But he did plan what he did to you, and he did plan to get rid of me! How can you excuse him?"

"I am not simply wiping it all away, Katie. Of course he must give an account of all the harm he has done these past weeks. We can forgive him, but he must still bear the consequences of these terrible wrongs—to us and to Laila as well. But the events of long ago must not haunt the present. Lars's empty room has been the place where I have sought and found the refuge of God's presence as I might not have otherwise."

Katie stood silent, shaken by the answer spoken so simply, and watched Andrew put his arm around his aunt and draw her into a comforting embrace.

Then he said, "I'm going to climb those steps and see where they come out on top. Katie, there's plenty of room in there. Will you follow me in and hold the light until I get started up?"

Katie inched her way cautiously into the narrow opening on her hands and knees. She took the flashlight and watched him climb easily and quickly, reaching with his hands to pull himself up each step as though he were on a ladder. In a moment he was out of sight.

Then she flashed the light around the miniature cave, surprised at how large it was, and wondered how far back it went under the hillside. She shivered then at the thought of what dark secret acts the cold rocks had witnessed. The thought made her back out quickly into the cold, bright sunshine and stand beside Mrs. Sieverson looking out over the restless water.

They turned as Andrew came running along the shore, looking at his watch as he came up to them, his breath coming in gasps.

"I—timed myself. Took me—one minute—to go

up—the steps. Almost—eight—to come the way—we always did."

He stopped to get his breath and then asked, "Did you see me crawl out up there?"

Mrs. Sieverson shook her head. "No, we couldn't see you at all."

"How did you get out?" Katie asked.

"When I got to the top step inside, I felt around and discovered that the ground is cut out in a big circle like a—well, like a manhole cover that you see covering the sewer hole in the streets. All I had to do was push up and lift it out and crawl out."

"Could we have seen you if we had been up there in the house?"

He shook his head. "I doubt it. The exit is cut close behind the stone wall at the edge of the property. And of course the weeds and brush and stunted evergreen trees makes it look like a small jungle out there." He looked at Katie with a smile. "As you know," he added.

She nodded, remembering how frightening the scene had seemed when she had first looked down on it.

"That explains how Barry got away. Now the question is, where is he? Perhaps the police have some word by now." Mrs. Sieverson's voice was laced with sadness as she added, "Andrew, I cannot help thinking of his mother.

They turned and walked back along the shore. What Barry had done was becoming clearer, but not why. Katie thought of all the questions that still

243

needed answers and wondered if they would ever untangle all the twisted strings.

"This explains all the burglaries so many years ago," Mrs. Sieverson said as they walked along the street toward home, her voice still tight with strain and tiredness. She explained to Katie.

"The Jorgenson house was robbed several times, and the burglars melted into thin air. Other homes found valuable items gone in spite of locked doors. I saw Barry once with a little round paperweight, a beautiful little thing, though not valuable, that I had given to a friend across the street. She kept it in her bedroom on her dressing table. After her house was burglarized, my friend told me that was one of the items she most regretted losing. They moved away soon after. A few weeks later I saw Barry tossing the paperweight in the air, playing catch with it. He claimed he had found it, looking at me with those clear eyes that seemed always so guileless. And of course he could have. The burglars could have discarded it as of no value. But I wondered—especially later after Lars was gone."

Katie heard again Barry's boast, "I have keys to all the houses."

The grim note still in his voice, Andrew, said, "It was using those steps that made him able to get away so fast the other night when he broke into the house."

"And that explains how he could be standing in the trees watching the house, and a few minutes later be at the front door with something he had just

244

picked up fresh from the shore," Katie remembered.

Andrew unlocked the front door and stood aside for them to enter. "I am going to call again to see if there is word of him yet. All exits from the city are being watched, of course—highways, the airport, even the bus station, although that is not the way Barry would choose to travel."

His eyes narrowed. "If he tries to hitchhike, he may get away, because we have no way to check every motorist. The police have a description of him, but we know he is good at disguising himself. We can only pity the person who gives him a lift."

"He wouldn't necessarily harm—" Katie began. She stopped when Andrew answered, "He'll want a car. Not his own."

He looked down at his aunt still standing in the open doorway, her small figure showing indecision. "Coming?"

She stood irresolute, looking over at the Jorgenson house. "Andrew, I am going over to Inga."

His eyes were anxious. "Is that wise?"

"I do not know. But years ago we were friends. She has never been anything else to me. She protected me as a child. Now she needs my protection."

Andrew and Katie stood together on the steps, watching her slender figure start down the driveway. Then she changed her direction and struck off across the brown grass. As she neared the grove of trees, Andrew grasped Katie's arm and gave a smothered exclamation. "Look!"

A woman's figure left the shelter of the trees and took several halting steps forward. The two women met, reached their arms at the same time, and clung together.

After a few moments, they saw Mrs. Sieverson turn and beckon. Andrew said, "Stay here," and strode away across the brown hard ground. Katie watched them stand together talking and then followed their slow progress back, one on each side giving support to the fragile frame. When they reached the wide shallow front steps, Andrew picked up Mrs. Jorgenson and carried her into the house and up the stairs to Mrs. Sieverson's room.

"Katie, get a heating pad from that bottom dresser drawer and then run down and fix some hot tea, will you please?" Mrs. Sieverson pulled back the eiderdown as she spoke and adjusted the pillows.

Andrew followed Katie as she hurried down the stairs. He went into the study, and she heard him dial a number and say, "Officer Wilson? Bring a couple of men. We know where Jorgenson is."

She waited a moment just inside the louvered kitchen doors and listened to his footsteps as he went back upstairs. Were they still in danger from Barry? She felt again the quiet of the house. It seemed to her that it had a waiting feel as though time were suspended. She filled the teakettle and set it on the stove to heat, and then got out a delicate cup and saucer and a dainty napkin, trying to do what Mrs. Sieverson would do for her dearest friend.

Andrew came back downstairs and went into the kitchen. His face showed strain.

She looked across at him. "I heard what you told the police. Where is he?"

"At home."

"Won't he get away before the police come?"

Andrew shook his head. "He is asleep in his room, and his mother locked the door. She said she has suspected all along that something was not quite right in Barry. That's what has made an invalid out of her all these years. She refused to face the reality that something was psychologically wrong with him. She shut it out of her mind by shutting herself off from life. To think that he might have harmed Lars was more than she could accept."

Andrew's voice choked, and he waited a moment. "When Barry came home this morning after his father had left for the office and asked for her help, he talked wildly about Aunt Sigrid. His words were incoherent, but from what he did say his mother thought he had harmed his aunt. That decided her. She told him to get some sleep, that she would help him. He had no idea that this was the help she would choose for him—turning him in to keep him from doing any more harm to himself as well as others."

The teakettle's incessant, sharp whistle cut into the conversation. Katie filled the little hand-painted blue-flowered teapot. Andrew took the tray she fixed and followed her through the hall. As they reached the foot of the stairs, the door chimes rang. Giving

247

her the tray, Andrew opened the door to two policemen. He turned to Katie, his voice low.

"I will go over with them. It may be some time before I get back. My aunt will keep Mrs. Jorgenson here until it is all over."

Katie went upstairs with the tray and tapped lightly on the closed bedroom door. She expected to find the room quiet and dark, the curtains and shades tightly drawn. But when Mrs. Sieverson opened the door, she saw sunlight highlighting the sparkle of the cut glass jars on Mrs. Sieverson's dressing table and reflecting on the gloss of the furniture. Music poured smoothly from a record player across the room. She could see Mrs. Jorgenson half-hidden in the highbacked green velvet chair by the window, her thin, blue-veined hands resting on the chair arms. The only evidence of sadness was in the tears that streaked Mrs. Sieverson's cheeks. She smiled at Katie and took the tray with a quiet, "Thank you, my dear."

The door chimes rang again. Katie hurried down and opened the door to Jane.

"Katie, I can't stay, but I had to find out if you really are all right. Mark is waiting in the car because we really are in a hurry. I just wanted to explain why we were out front that afternoon when I said I would be in the lab for hours."

"You don't really owe me an explanation," Katie began.

"Yes, I do. We were worried about you and didn't dare let on to you. I said a policeman had asked about you, but that was really later. What brought us out was a seedy looking character who came around asking all kinds of questions about you."

Barry, Katie's mind said positively.

"Mark said we should hunt up this Barry fellow and tell him to keep an eye on you so we drove out. Then when we got here, his house looked so—well, unlived in, that we thought we had the wrong house. Mark decided he would check on you so he drove by lots of times. We felt responsible for you since I had urged you to move here. After all, we're friends, and old friends are the best friends. That's a—"

"Quote from Mark," Katie finished, smiling at her affectionately. "Jane, tell Mark thanks so much. And, please, come back. I want Mrs. Sieverson and Andrew to meet you."

"We will. I'm dying to hear about this whole mystery, and Mark wants to see the house. By the way, what I said about him is true. He really did drive around as a kid and look at all the fancy houses."

Katie watched Jane hurry down the driveway. Andrew's car turned in, and Jane stopped as he leaned to speak to her. He pulled up then beside the house and came in. A smile lifted his somber expression as he saw Katie.

He sobered instantly and shrugged out of his coat, dropping it on a chair as he walked through the long living-room to stand at the window.

"Well, Barry has admitted his part in all that has happened, though we are still left with unanswered questions."

"What made him start this all over again? I mean, bringing up all that had happened in the past?"

"Apparently he thought Laila had stumbled onto something. She must have made some remark to him about a 'so-called accidental drowning.' It scared him, even after all these years. He decided there must be evidence in the house and that he would get it. Of course, there is a lot we don't know yet. Some of this I'm guessing from pieces both he and Laila have said. His plan included getting Laila locked away on a counterfeiting charge so she would forget about what had happened in the past."

"But how does all this fit together? Why would Barry get mixed up in the counterfeit thing? He told me he was independently wealthy."

Andrew nodded. "He is. Not having to work has always been part of his problem. He claims he was born lazy, and I think there is truth to it. He could have been a great swimmer, possibly even Olympic quality, but it took too much effort. He could have been spectacular in business, but he couldn't stand the nine-to-five grind. He wasted himself, his time, his potential. Then he found that Laila dated a man who had done time for counterfeiting, and offered to back the fellow. He was an American with some connections in Mexico. Since Barry was in this just for fun, he decided to add a little flair to the adventure by putting coded messages in a book."

"My Mexican War history book!"

"Exactly. And Barry saw you take the notes out—"

Katie shook her head. "He wasn't there. I'm sure of that. Of course, I hadn't met him then, but I would have remembered. The only person near me was an old man reading a newspaper who was annoyed when I bumped him." She stopped at Andrew's expression, and added incredulously, "Barry?"

"Possibly. Probably."

"But—I would have recognized him later."

"Not necessarily. I suspect he has a closet full of disguises."

"But why involve me? He *knew* I was not a part of it."

Andrew shrugged. "To add more spice to the game—and to cause someone trouble. I'm speculating now, of course, but if he was in the library and saw me talk to you at the desk, it would be like him to adapt his plans to play a trick. Like calling me about the pretty librarian," he finished with a quick smile. "But of course it wasn't a nice trick, because it caused you so much trouble." He looked across at her gravely. "The only good thing that came out of it was that it brought you here."

She had to answer honestly the questioning note in his voice. "I am glad, too, now." She saw the light in his eyes and the involuntary step toward her that he checked. Honesty made her say, "I have been angry at you for your suspicions, though now I can see why you had them. I couldn't seem to convince you that all the evidence Laila and Barry planted was not really evidence."

"Laila said it was all Barry's idea, even sending the bills to your bank. I don't know, and she says she doesn't either, how he discovered your account number."

Katie frowned, thinking back over the times she had been with Barry, and remembered. "I left my bag in the car once when I came into the house to leave my books. He must have searched it then."

They stood in silence, watching the waves wash up on the rocks far below. "Will we ever know why he did it?" Katie asked.

Andrew shook his head. "There is never an easy, simple explanation for a quirk like this in a person's makeup. Of course the ultimate answer is that Barry never yielded to God's authority over him."

He turned to look out the other window across at the Jorgenson house. His voice was heavy as he talked. "He sat through the same church services and camping trips and meetings and parties all the rest of us did. But everything he heard apparently rolled right off him."

Katie thought about Barry sitting in church Sunday—yesterday—his eyes intent on the minister, singing hymns with such enjoyment, his smile flashing a greeting to everyone who spoke to him.

"None of us really cared about him."

Katie made an involuntary sound of protest, but he shook it away and repeated, "We didn't care. Not really. If we had, we would have been more aware of him, *tried* to be friends. Instead we turned him off. When he did the silly, or goofy, or cruel things, we either said tolerantly, 'Oh, well, that's Barry, always needing attention,' or else we got mad at him. None of us really cared about him. I should have; I was older."

Katie saw his jaw muscles tighten with the effort of keeping his husky voice steady.

252

"It isn't too late, is it? Can't you still talk to him, get through to him?"

He looked at her over his shoulder, hope creeping into his eyes. "Yes, this may be the time he can be reached. I've given up on him so many times before. Maybe God is giving him—and me—another chance."

Another chance? Was there one? Could her parents—?

The question was terribly important, but she found it hard to ask. Then she saw Andrew take a step toward her, his voice gentle and questioning. "How about it, Katie? Have you ever given God room in your life?"

Out of the terrible ache in her throat, she managed to say, "I'm thinking of my parents. Of their goodness, their gentleness. Is that all gone? Is there no chance for them?"

"That's a choice that comes in this life only, Katie."

His voice was low and so terribly kind that it brought the tears she had been struggling to hold back.

She listened as he went on in that same voice, "Don't pass by the decision for yourself. All that has happened these past weeks would have no meaning if some good doesn't come from it. I believe your coming here was part of God's design for you all along. The ugliness of Barry's actions is a black thread running through the design, but a necessary thread. It brought you to us."

He waited a moment and said, "You can't answer

for your parents. If you know my aunt's story, you know she struggled with that sorrow for years, and finally had to leave it in the hands of an all-wise God. You will have to do that too. There may have been open doors they could have taken and didn't. If so, that is terribly sad, and I am sorry. But don't let that keep you from accepting God's salvation. Jesus Christ is the way to God, the only way. Has all that my aunt lived before you these weeks shown you that? Can you believe that?"

Katie looked back into the intensity of his clear blue eyes. The expression she had seen in them the first time they met was there again, warm, friendly, loving.

She reached her hand to him. "I want to believe it, but I still have questions."

"We'll help you find the answers," he said, and took her hand in his.

Moody Press, a ministry of the Moody Bible Institute, is designed for education, evangelization, and edification. If we may assist you in knowing more about Christ and the Christian life, please write us without obligation: Moody Press, c/o MLM, Chicago, Illinois 60610.

254

61672